MUMSHOP

CECI JENKINSON

ff

faber and faber

First published in 2008
by Faber and Faber Limited
3 Queen Square London WC1N 3AU

Printed in England
by CPI Bookmarque, Croydon

A CIP record for this book
is available from the British Library

ISBN 978-0-571-23950-4

2 4 6 8 10 9 7 5 3 1

For Harry and Bertie

CONTENTS

As Cool as a Cowboy

'I'm not coming down and that's final!' shouted Tara from inside the tree house.

Oli Biggles glared up into the tree. 'When I've been brainwashed to death, I'll come back and haunt you!' he yelled.

'Good! I'll like you much better as a ghost!'

Little sisters, Oli decided bitterly, were the jellyfish in the sea of life.

Oli wandered down to the end of the garden. It was a beautiful spring afternoon but his reason for wanting to be at the end of the garden was not to admire the floating April clouds or the beams of golden sunshine. These things floated and beamed unnoticed by Oli. His reason for wanting to be at the end of the garden was simply that it was further away from the house than anywhere else he could go.

And Oli's reason for wanting to be as far away from the house as possible was that within it there lurked a mum of the most dreadful kind. If there was ever a World's Worst Mum Competition, Oli felt sure that this mum would be up there on the highest podium with a gold medal round her neck.

You see, earlier that day Oli took his own mum to the Mum Shop and swapped her for a new one. It was all because of an argument. A tame, well-behaved argument at first:

'ALL my friends get to watch *Real Blood Bath Murders*, so why can't I?'

'Because I'm not ALL your friends' mothers.'

But then somehow the argument escaped and ran wild:

'I wish you were,' he shouted. 'I wish I had a different mum.' As soon as the words were out of his mouth Oli wished he could catch them all and cram them back in. For a moment there was silence, but it was the silence of a hand-grenade flying through the air. Oli braced himself for the blast.

'Well, in that case,' said his Mum, 'You'd

better take me to the Mum Shop,' and she went upstairs to pack.

The Mum Shop? For a second Oli was alarmed but then he realised his mum was bluffing. She did this sort of thing sometimes, when she was really cross. He remembered the day she turfed him and Tara out of the car to walk home because they would not stop fighting in the back. She just left them on the pavement and drove away. They were stunned. They finally started walking and after a dozen paces they found her waiting round the next corner. Then there was the time she handed them over to the police at a fairground because they had wandered off and got lost. The policeman locked them up in a mobile cell – with bars – for a whole minute. This gave them such a shock that they had been little angels for at least half an hour afterwards. This time it would be just the same: Mum would go on for as long as possible pretending there really was a place where you could hand in your mum, just to teach him a lesson. Well, this time he was not going to be stunned *or* shocked.

He was going to be as cool as a cowboy.

Oli heard Mum knocking on his older sister Becky's bedroom door. Knockers on Becky's door needed cast-iron knuckles if they were going to be heard over her stereo.

'Oli's taking me to the Mum Shop,' called Mum. 'Keep an eye on Tara till I get back. She's in the tree house.'

'OK, Mum,' called Becky. 'Have fun.'

Oli rolled his eyes. You couldn't get Becky to

listen to anything unless you used key words like boyfriend, new clothes or pop star.

Mum came down with her suitcase. It looked heavy, which meant that she had not just taken it out of the cupboard to use for effect, but had actually packed it. 'Well, come on then,' she said.

She led the way to the nearby bus stop, where they waited in silence for the Number 11.

How long is she going to keep this up? wondered Oli as the bus arrived and the doors clattered open. He glanced at the man behind the wheel and nearly fell over when he saw that it was Mr Grimble. Only last week Oli had been dared by his best friend Skipjack Haynes to ask this very driver – an enormous hairy man with huge teeth – for two tickets to the planet Mars. Mr Grimble had risen up and roared at them like King Kong. 'I'll get you further away than Mars – with my right boot!' he had boomed, shaking a fist as big as a boxing glove. The boys had fled for their lives, in front of a whole busload of goggling passengers and with Mr Grimble shouting all sorts of threats after them. Oli had been having nightmares ever since, really

scary ones of being chased through the jungle by an angry Mr Grimble in a leopard-skin loincloth.

So now Oli stood behind his mum, hoping not to be recognised. Mr Grimble glared down at them. Surely Mum wasn't going to ask him if his bus went to the Mum Shop?

'Does your bus go to the Mum Shop?' asked Mum. Much as Oli wished she would stop this crazy bluff, he had to admit she was brave. He was shaking in his size-five cheesies as he waited for King Kong to shout at them.

'We do indeed,' replied Mr Grimble. 'We stop right outside their front door. Hop on.' Oli was puzzled but then he decided that Mum must have tipped Mr G a secret wink.

Mum heaved her suitcase on to the bus and paid the fare. Oli climbed on after her, pretending to scratch the side of his face closest to Mr Grimble.

There came a menacing growl: 'Just a moment, young man.' Oli stopped, still scratching, heart thumping.

'Aren't you going to help your mum with her luggage?' demanded Mr Grimble.

Oli mumbled something and with his free hand he took the case from his mum. It weighed more than a fossilised grand piano. 'Wow, Mum!' he exclaimed. 'What have you got in here?'

'Books,' Mum replied. 'I might have time to read, for once.'

The bus rattled along its usual route and stopped at all the usual places where all the usual sorts of people climbed on and off. Mum looked out of the window. Oli sighed and slumped further down in his seat. How long was she going to keep this up?

'Next stop Mum Shop,' bellowed Mr Grimble. The bus shuddered to a halt just as a big black sign loomed up in front of Oli's window:

'Replacement Mother Agency'.

Oli sat up, stunned and shocked.

'That's us,' said Mum, standing.

His mind whirling, Oli clambered down from the bus. What? How? Why? Thoughts flew around inside his head like sweet wrappers in a hurricane. Mum led the way up a tidy path, with Oli trailing behind in a daze. A real, live Mum Shop? In this town? Mum stopped before a plain white house with a plain black door and rang the bell.

I'm dreaming, thought Oli. That's it. I'm not really here at all – I'm far away on Planet Gonk, tucked up in bed. All this is just a bad dream. I'll pinch myself and then I'll wake up.

So Oli shut his eyes tight and pinched his arm hard, but when he looked again he was still standing in front of the plain black door with his mum and a suitcase full of books.

A buzzer sounded from inside. 'In we go,' said Mum cheerfully. But as he followed her into the house, Oli's heart was beating like the bongos of a Zulu chief's chief bongo beater summoning the tribe to war.

The Mum Shop was just as neat inside as out. The white hall was arranged like a dentist's waiting room, with a row of grey chairs, exactly spaced, and a tall green potted plant which stood quietly in one corner.

Behind a long counter was an office area with a grey computer desk at the front and a grey sheet covering something very big in the middle. As big, in fact, as an elephant-smuggler's crate. Behind the grey desk sat a thin young man engrossed in sharpening a pencil.

Mum sat on a grey chair and looked at Oli expectantly. Oli wondered why she was so relaxed. Then, with a painful swell of anger, he knew why. She doesn't believe I'll go through with it, he thought. She thinks I'll bottle out at the last minute. Well, Mum, you're wrong. I'm braver than you think – watch this.

Blinded by a flash of pride, Oli marched to the counter.

The young man behind the desk stood up.

'Can I help you?' he asked in a reedy voice.

He was as thin as a rat's tail, with a long throat, greasy black hair and a beaky nose. On his black jacket was pinned a label informing all who wished to know – and any who did not – that he was Cedric Stringfellow. Oli was reminded of a picture he had once seen of a scraggy seabird that had been bobbing up and down on its wave in the North Sea, dreaming of fish, when it had been bagged from behind by an oil slick.

'I said, can I help you?' repeated Cedric Stringfellow, a little crossly.

For a moment Oli was completely distracted by the Adam's apple that shot up and down the man's endless throat like a frog in a sock. He tore his eyes from the bouncing amphibian to the pale face above and searched his head for something to say. Cedric Stringfellow clicked his tongue impatiently and asked,

'Is that your mother over there?'

'Er, yes,' stammered Oli, not looking round at his mum.

'So you've come to make an exchange?'

'Er, yes, no, er . . .'

'Well? Which is it?' demanded Cedric Stringfellow. Oli took a deep breath.

'Yes,' he said loudly.

Cedric Stringfellow opened a cupboard door to reveal a panel covered with numbered buzzers. Below each buzzer hung a key. He took one of the keys off its hook and waved it in the air. 'The room number is on the key,' he called out to Oli's mum. 'Through the double doors and up the stairs to the first floor. You may go straight there and start filling out the necessary forms.'

Mum took the key and carried her case to the swing doors. She turned to look at Oli. 'See you soon,' she said. Then she was gone, and the doors swung emptily to and fro.

2

Oli Meets the Matcher

Oli Biggles swallowed what felt like a large
conker that had got stuck in his throat.

Just then the front door was flung open and a
pink flurry burst into the Mum Shop.

'I've really had enough of you this time,
Mum!' screamed the pink flurry.

'I've had enough of *you*, an' all!' yelled the
blonde woman who tottered in after her
on red shoes with dagger
heels.

'I can't wait to get
rid of you!'

'Likewise!'
shouted the woman
and she stuck her
tongue out at her
daughter.

Wow – a Mum from Hell, thought Oli. He looked with sympathy at the flurry of pink, who had come to a standstill and was now a girl, quite pretty, of about his own age. She stormed past him, banged the counter with her fist and shouted, 'Hey, Cecil! I want to swap my horrible Mum!'

Cedric Stringfellow looked down his nose at mother and daughter. 'My name,' he announced coldly, 'is not Cecil, it's Cedric.'

The girl tossed her head. 'As if I care what your stupid name is. Just get me a new mum, will you?'

Cedric pursed his thin lips so tightly they disappeared altogether and handed the girl a form and a pencil. 'Here you are,' he said, 'again. But you are running out of choices.'

'So what,' replied the girl. 'Anyone's better than her.' She began to fill in the form.

'Oi, Cecil,' called the woman, 'make sure she gets Snow White's step-mum, poisoned apple and all.'

Oli was busy gawping at both the girl and the mother when Cedric Stringfellow passed him a sheet of blue paper headed Replacement Mother Application Form and he remembered where he was. Now that he had handed in his own mum, he supposed he had better get an exchange. It might even be a laugh to try out a new mum for a day or two, as long as it wasn't for ever . . .

'I could get my own mum back, right?' he asked Cedric Stringfellow. 'I mean, if I ever had to?'

'Your mother certainly seemed to think so,' sniffed Cedric. 'But it's nothing to do with me. The Matcher must decide.'

'The Matcher?'

Cedric Stringfellow flapped an arm at the grey-sheeted elephant-smuggler's crate in the middle of the room.

'The Matcher decides everything here.'

'Why is he under a sheet?' asked Oli.

'You'll see. Fill out this form, please. You must tell the truth and you must use capital letters. You know what capital letters are, I suppose?'

Oli rolled his eyes. 'Duh-h, I'm not sure, are they the big ones or the likkle ones?'

'The big ones. And then sign your name here, here and here,' continued Cedric Stringfellow, jabbing the paper with a twiggy finger.

The girl rapped on the counter impatiently. 'Look, Cecil, are you gonna send my mum away through them doors or not?' she demanded. Cedric tutted, took another key from the cupboard and held it out.

'At last!' exclaimed the girl.

'Likewise!' retorted the mother, grabbing the key and marching to the double doors.

'I hope you get matched with someone really HORRIBLE!' the girl yelled after her.

'LIKEWISE!' shouted the mother and she stormed through the doors.

'What are you staring at?' demanded the girl. Oli hurriedly turned his attention to the form, but despite his best attempts to concentrate, his mind kept tiptoeing back to the Matcher. He longed to peek under the sheet. What would he find? He imagined an ancient wise man, very shrivelled, sitting cross-legged on a mat. Oli was just wishing for X-ray eyes when Cedric pulled off the sheet.

Underneath was an enormous, multicoloured machine.

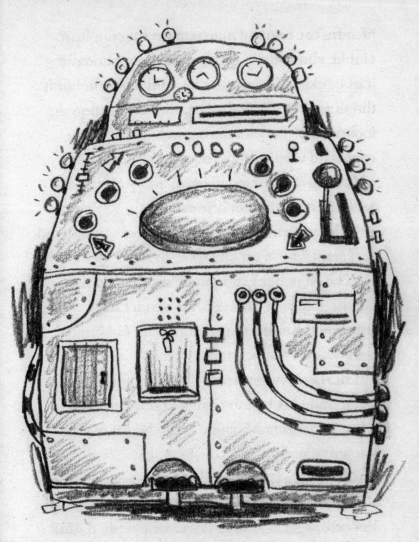

'That's the Matcher?' asked Oli in disbelief.
'Of course,' replied Cedric. 'What did you
expect?' He pushed a bright red button the size

of a frisbee and the machine gave a couple of clunks, shook itself gently and started humming and blinking. It might be big, Oli decided, but it did not look very high-tech. In fact the more he looked at it, the more it reminded him of the robots he used to make out of egg boxes and bottle tops, covered with dials and switches and every part a different colour.

'What a strange machine,' he said. 'Where did you get it?'

'The Matcher was built by my grandfather,' Cedric told him proudly. 'He was a Great Inventor. He used the engine of an old jumbo jet.'

Oli was very surprised that Cedric could be related to anyone interesting enough to make a Mum Matching Machine from the spare parts of an aeroplane.

'How does it work?' he asked.

'It contains a brilliant data system linked to the computer on the desk,' Cedric replied. 'But the details are top secret. I am the only person in the world who knows how to operate it.'

'What's that bit?' Oli asked, pointing to a

small tap just below a steaming air vent.

'That's a built-in tea-maker,' said Cedric. 'Grandad put that in when he was installing the cooling system. He loved a nice cup of tea.'

'And that?' Oli pointed to a small yellow door, complete with tiny keyhole, and stamped with the words DANGER! KEEP OUT in big red letters.

'That's the built-in biscuit tin.'

The pink girl waved her form at Cedric. 'Make it snappy, Cecil. I want my new mum to take me shopping before closing time.'

Cedric took the form and fed it into a wide slot in the Matcher. Then he flicked a switch marked 'Turbo Boost'.

'Ooh,' said Oli, interested. The machine began to chug and rattle like an ancient tractor, wheezing as if climbing a very steep hill. This wasn't quite what Oli expected, but a machine that ancient probably took a lot of warming up. Any minute now, he thought, the Turbo Boost bit will begin. But with a loud gurgle and a burp of black smoke, the Matcher stopped altogether.

'Oh!' said Oli, disappointed, for it seemed that

the Matcher would be matching no more. The pink girl would be stuck with Likewise and he would never get to see *Real Blood Bath Murders*. But then there came through the silence a low drone which grew and grew until the room was filled with noise and wind. A burst of lights cascaded across the machine which began to shake like a huge spin-dryer.

'Wow!' said Oli, glued. The girl looked bored. She had seen it all before.

The roar grew even louder and the rattling more violent. The lights flashed crazily and clouds of steam and smoke billowed out of air vents.

'I think it's going to take off, or explode,' shouted Oli over the din.

'Nonsense,' Cedric said. 'The Matcher would never do anything so silly.'

Then, just as Oli was about to dive for cover, everything stopped. Silence filled the room. A small white card popped out of the Matcher and fluttered to the ground.

'The Matcher has decided,' announced Cedric grandly, picking up the card. 'Mother 33.'

'Let's see it – give it here!' cried the girl.

Cedric handed her the card and opened the cupboard to press the buzzer for her new mum.

'How long will she be?' demanded the girl.

'How on earth should I know?' snapped Cedric. 'It's Mother 33 you're waiting for, not Big Ben.'

Offended, the girl turned her back on Cedric and crossed her arms to wait. Cedric took a screwdriver from one of the desk drawers and began tightening some of the Matcher's bolts. The show was over. For the first time since he had arrived at the Mum Shop, Oli was able to give his full attention to filling in his Replacement Mother Application Form.

This was simple enough to start with. Part One was called 'About You'. Oli filled in his name, address and age (eleven) and listed his hobbies as go-karting and being a secret agent. Part Two was 'Your Family'. Oli started with Becky (age – fourteen; hobbies – pop music and boyfriends) but when he came to Tara (age – ten) he realised he was going to have a bit of trouble with the hobbies section. The most truthful entry would have been 'rescuing animals and dissecting them if they die' but he was worried that this would put off all but the strangest mothers. In the end he wrote 'wildlife and science'.

The swing doors at the back of the room now opened and a fair-haired woman in pink came through. She smiled brightly at the girl. 'Hi!' she squealed. 'You must be Chardonnay! Let's go shopping!'

Well, that was a good match, thought Oli as he watched the pair leave arm in arm, chatting and giggling. He went on with the form, encouraged by this proof of the Matcher's skill.

In Part Three he had to explain in fewer than ten words why he was returning his own mother. After much counting on his fingers Oli wrote, 'She wouldn't let me watch *Real Blood Bath Murders*'. Finally he had to list three Replacement Mother Requirements. That was easy.

> 1 Pizza twice a day
> 2 As much TV as I want
> 3 Lots of fun

Oli handed his finished form to Cedric. As he watched it disappear into the slot he began to feel quite excited. Perhaps he'd get a totally perfect mum, who'd let him do anything he wanted! Oli hardly noticed the Matcher's jet-propelled routine this time; his imagination had lifted him to a wonderland of all-night telly and pizza for breakfast.

Out popped the white card.

'The Matcher has decided,' announced Cedric.

'Well?' demanded Oli impatiently. 'Who have I got?'

Cedric handed him the card. Oli read aloud: 'HA HA NO CHANCE DREAM ON'.

'What does that mean?'

'It means,' Cedric said with great satisfaction, 'that your requirements were not realistic. You will have to start all over again.'

So Oli, with a sigh, changed his pizza requirement from twice a day to once a day. He handed the form back to Cedric and kept his fingers crossed while he waited for the Matcher to do its stuff. At last the little white card flew out.

'The Matcher has decided,' proclaimed Cedric, picking up the card. 'You have been given Mother 295.'

'Who is Mother 295?' asked Oli. To his astonishment Cedric was almost smiling.

'She is an excellent choice,' Cedric assured him as he pressed the numbered buzzer. A new spring in the young man's step made Oli feel uneasy. Why was he so cheerful all of a sudden?

'In what way is it an excellent choice?' he asked.

'Every choice the Matcher makes is excellent,' replied Cedric. 'Do sit down while you're waiting. I am sure she won't be long.'

As Oli waited for Mother 295 to appear, a notice on the wall behind the counter caught his eye: 'Immediate Payment required for Replacement Mothers'. Payment? Help! Oli scrabbled in his trouser pocket and pulled out a collection of small coins, rubber bands and toast crumbs. He did some quick adding up: 25 p. Double help.

'Er, Cedric,' said Oli, 'I didn't notice that pink girl paying you for her new mum . . .?'

'She didn't pay cash. She has an account.'

'An account?'

'She's a regular customer. We send her a bill every month.'

'Oh, I see. Er, Cedric,' Oli took a deep breath, 'I'm afraid I didn't bring any money. I left home in a bit of a hurry, you see.'

'Don't worry,' Cedric reassured him. 'The mother you have chosen is free. Absolutely free.

Call it a special offer. An extra-special offer, in fact.'

'Wow! That's lucky!' exclaimed Oli. He began to think he had judged Cedric unfairly. The poor man looked like a strangled vulture but he was really a very polite and generous fellow.

Then the double doors opened and in came Mother 295.

3
Ping Yong Police and Pepperoni Pizza

'Hiya, Oli!' shouted Mother 295, leaping forwards with a huge orange backpack bouncing about behind her and a hand like a shovel outstretched in front. 'I'm Sid. Gimme five!'

Speechless, Oli held out his hand which was slapped with such hearty force that his whole arm nearly came off. Sid guffawed. 'Don't worry, Oli, you'll get used to my little ways! Come on, let's get out of this zombie house! Cheerio, Cedric and mind you don't smile – might crack your face!'

She squeezed her backpack out through the doorway and set off up the path at a brisk pace. 'I am just so glad to get away from that lemon Cedric,' she shouted over her shoulder. 'Now then, are we bussing it home?' She came to such a sudden halt at the bus stop that Oli, who had been hurrying to keep up, bumped straight into her backpack. Sid guffawed again. 'Watch out, Oli – at this rate we'll be wanting an ambulance, not a bus – ha-ha! Now, what number?'

'Number 11,' mumbled Oli, rubbing his nose.

'Smashing! My lucky number!' boomed Sid. She swung her backpack off her shoulders and on to the ground with a thud. 'Bet I spot it first,' and she propped her bottom on one of the bus stop bottom-props and squinted up the street, concentrating hard. Oli leant against the wall for a moment to let the fullness of Sid sink in.

Because full Sid was – full of noise and full of, well, *size*, thought Oli as he cast a sideways glance at her. Bright orange jeans and T-shirt, a halo of wildly curly orange hair and a backpack as big as a telephone box all combined to give a general effect of enormousness. So did the voice, like an elephant in full trumpet.

'Look – a number 11!' yelled Sid, pointing. 'I win, I win!'

As the bus shuddered to a halt, Oli shot a glance at the driver and was relieved to see that it was not Mr Grimble. Getting on a bus with Sid was bad enough without having Mr Grimble to worry about.

The bus was very full and they had to stand. Oli looked around at all the normal people sitting on the bus who were quietly reading or looking out of the window. He hoped that Sid would not be embarrassing. Sid, however, had fallen silent for the first time; she was watching some passengers near the back of the bus. Looking at her, Oli decided that she was quite unlike anyone he had ever met and he was suddenly curious.

'How long have you been at the Mum Shop?' he asked.

Sid rolled her eyes. 'Too long! About two weeks, I think. I've been there before, though. I go back every couple of years, just to keep old Cedric on his toes – ha ha! And because it's free board and lodging. Not very good board and lodging, mind you, but free. I go there for a little holiday.'

She was once again looking towards the back of the bus. Oli followed her gaze and saw an old man fast asleep and a young woman in smart office clothes reading a book. He wondered why Sid should find this pair so interesting.

'And where do you go otherwise?' he asked. 'To different families?'

'Now and then,' said Sid. 'I try not to get picked very often but I think Cedric hands me out for free sometimes just to get rid of me.'

She must have noticed Oli's face turn red because she added hastily, 'Not this time, of course. For once the Matcher has got it absolutely right. I could tell as soon as I saw you. We're going to be a smashing team!' These

reassuring words were underlined by a hearty
back-slap that sent Oli lurching into the person
standing in front of him.

When he was upright again and had finished
apologising, he said, 'So, you're not a real mum
at all?'

'Yes, I am, or at least I was. I'm just
completely hopeless at it. It's a shame, really, 'cos
I love being with nice kids like you.' She sighed.
'But sooner or later disaster always strikes.'

Somehow this did not surprise Oli. He had
the feeling that wherever Sid went, disaster
would not be far behind, lurking in the shadows,
waiting to pounce.

'So I go travelling instead,' Sid went on.
'Globe-trotting with my trusty backpack. There
aren't many places I haven't seen or many jobs I
haven't done, I can tell you.'

'But why does Cedric let you use the Mum
Shop like a hotel?' Oli asked.

Sid gave one of her sudden loud guffaws
which made several of the passengers jump. The
old man went on sleeping. The smart young
woman went on reading her book. Sid winked

and leaned closer to Oli. 'I'd tell you my secret, but then I'd have to kill you,' she whispered.

'You'd find it really hard to kill me,' Oli whispered back. 'I'm training to be a secret agent.'

'Good for you! I've never been a secret agent but my last job was with the Ping Yong police force,' Sid told him proudly.

'The what?'

'You must have heard of the Ping Yong police force? The best police force in the world?'

'Er, no,' said Oli. He began to wonder whether Sid was living in a fantasy world.

The bus drew to a halt and the young woman with the book stood up. As she came down the aisle Sid suddenly put a hand on her shoulder.

The woman turned round. 'What are you doing?' she demanded.

'I'm stopping you,' said Sid cheerfully. Oli looked at her, horrified. What on earth was Sid doing now?'

'Let me go!' demanded the smart young woman. People were trying not to stare. The old man at the back of the bus was still asleep.

'Of course I'll let you go,' said Sid with a friendly smile. 'When you give me the wallet you've just stolen from that poor old man.' Now people were staring properly.

'Sid!' hissed Oli. 'What are you doing?'

'This is an outrage!' exclaimed the young woman. 'I insist that you let me go!'

'Sid! Please stop!' begged Oli. 'It's OK, I believe you about the Ping Yong police force. But you're not in Ping Yong now – you're on a Number 11 bus! And everyone is staring!'

'Help!' shrieked the young woman, struggling to free herself from Sid's grasp. 'I'm being attacked by a mad orange woman!'

'If you don't give that wallet back,' whispered Sid, 'you'll see just how mad this orange woman can be.'

Oli had just decided that this orange woman was completely mad and that he should jump off the bus and run away fast, when the young woman stopped struggling and pulled an old leather wallet from her bag. She slapped it on to Sid's hand and glared at her.

Sid let go of her shoulder. 'There. That wasn't too hard, was it? Now, buzz off and be a good girl.'

The young woman buzzed off. The whole bus exploded in a burst of clapping and cheering for Sid, who went very pink. People were shaking her warmly by the hand and asking her name. Oli changed his mind about running away. It was fun being on a bus with a superstar. The wallet was passed back down the bus and slipped into the pocket of the old man, who was still fast asleep.

When the fuss had died down Oli asked, 'But,

Sid, how did you know?'

Sid chuckled. 'You see it all in the Ping Yong police force, Oli my boy.'

'She didn't look like a criminal.'

'Oh yes, she did.'

The bus pulled up at Oli's home stop and they climbed off to a chorus of 'Goodbye, Sid!' As they approached the house Oli heard the shuffles and bounces of someone shooting basketball on the back patio. Becky never played ballgames for fear of chipping her fingernails so it had to be Tara, down from the tree house. The time had come to break the news about swapping mums. Tara was not going to be pleased.

'You go in, Sid,' Oli whispered, opening the front door for her. 'I'll just go and warn – and tell my sister you're here.'

'I'll come with you,' boomed Sid, 'and say hiya!'

'No, please don't! I mean, don't bother – I'll bring her straight in.' Oli disappeared round the side of the house. At the final corner he took a deep breath before coming face to face with . . .

'Skipjack! What are you doing here?'

Skipjack Haynes, best friend, Mr Grimble-teaser

and general trouble-magnet, shot the basketball through the hoop and turned round, grinning.

'Hi, Oli. I've thought of a plan to get our revenge on Mr Grimble for being so mean about our Mars joke. It's perfect – look.'

He picked up a large envelope, addressed in careful capitals to:

MISTER
GRIMBLE
THE BUS
STATION

He pulled out a sheet of paper and handed it to Oli.

The Town Hall
Thursday
Dear Mr Grimble,
KING-KONG-GRATULASHUNS!
You hav wun the King-Kong Look-
alike Computishun! You can cum and
get
yor grate prize from me on
Saterday. You must where this
badge so that the
town hall gards let you in.
From
The Mayor

Oli chuckled. 'And the badge?' he asked.

'Ah-ha. The badge is the best bit of all.'

With a proud flourish, Skipjack produced from the envelope a fluorescent green cardboard disc the size of a dinner plate. On it were four words in big black letters.

I AM
KING
KONG!

was grinning broadly. 'Can you imagine

mble turning up at the Town Hall

g that? Well? What do you think?'

'It's brilliant,' agreed Oli. 'There's just one problem.'

'What's that?'

'He might just guess that this letter isn't really from the mayor.'

'You mean my handwriting,' agreed Skipjack. 'That's why I'm here. We've got to type it so it looks official, and we can't do that at my house without someone spying on us. Your mum isn't as nosey as my mum.'

'Ah.' Pause. 'Skipjack, have you ever heard of the Mum Shop?'

His friend's eyes widened. 'You haven't been there?'

'How do you know about it?' asked Oli.

'Mum's always threatening to get us a replacement. So what happened?'

'I had an argument with Mum. She wouldn't let me watch *Real Blood Bath Murders*.'

'But no one's mum lets them watch *Real Blood Bath Murders*.'

'All the guys at school said they watched it,' objected Oli.

'They were lying.'

'You said you watched it, too.'

'I was lying.'

'Skipjack!'

Skipjack shrugged. 'Sometimes you have to. Anyway, I tried to wink at you so you'd realise. So you went and handed your mum in at the Mum Shop, just because of *Real Blood Bath Murders*?'

Oli was defensive. 'That and other things.'

'You're crazy. So have you got a replacement mum?'

Oli nodded.

'Wicked! Is she cool?'

Oli hesitated. 'Well, not cool, exactly. But she was in the Ping Yong police.'

'The *what*?'

'Well, she's travelled a lot. She's had loads of adventures. She's called Sid.'

'Sid?'

'Sid.'

'And is she going to let you watch *Real Blood Bath Murders*?'

'I don't know.'

'After all that, you don't know?' repeated Skipjack in disbelief.

'I forgot to ask her about that. And about the pizza,' added Oli, remembering. 'I made a special request at the Mum Shop for pizza every day,' he explained.

'Well, come on. Let's go and ask now.'

They found Sid in the kitchen, rummaging in the bottom of her backpack. The kitchen table was piled high with strange-looking tins and packages.

'Hi, Sid. This is Skipjack.'

Sid looked up, her orange hair bouncing and her face pink from being upside down.

'Hiya, Skipjack! Ah-ha, here it is.'

She sat back and held up a small green tin. 'Ulan tea,' she announced. 'Smashing stuff. Drank it all the time when I was living in my yurt in Outer Mongolia. Alone with my yak. Have a smell.'

She opened the tin and held it out. Oli sniffed gingerly and staggered backwards.

'It's a strong pong, eh?' agreed Sid. 'Let's get a brew on.'

'We only popped in to ask a couple of things . . .' said Oli hurriedly.

'Ask away,' said Sid. 'An electric kettle – what luxury. In Mongolia I had to use a tin pot over a fire made of dried yak's dung. It added an interesting flavour.' She sprinkled some tea leaves into a mug.

'Can we order a pizza for lunch and can we watch *Real Blood Bath Murders* tonight?'

Sid's face lit up. 'Is *Real Blood Bath Murders* on tonight? It's my best programme ever! And I love pizza – triple-pepperoni for me, please, and extra cheese. This is great – I can see I'm going to love it here!'

Sid happily poured boiling water into her mug and at once the kitchen was filled with a pungent steam that brought tears to the eyes. Oli grabbed the phone and the pizza leaflet and the boys ran back outside, holding their noses and laughing.

Mr Happy won't be Happy

'What d'you want on your pizza?' Oli asked
Skipjack once they could breathe again.

'The usual, please, Oli.' Skipjack picked up
the basketball and started bouncing it.

'Triple-pepperoni with pineapple and grated
chocolate?'

'That's the one.'

'I suppose I'd better get something for my
sisters. I haven't told them yet – about Sid, I
mean. I suppose I'd better do that too.' Oli
pictured the tree house and felt the shadow of
doom pass over him. 'I'll order the pizzas first,'
he decided. 'They can't give me a hard time if
I've got them pizza for lunch.'

'You're not afraid of your own sisters, are
you?' Skipjack asked.

'Not Becky, but Tara in a temper is even scarier than Mr Grimble.'

'But, she's smaller than you – and a *girl*!' laughed Skipjack.

'So is a Black Widow spider,' said Oli darkly. He started dialling.

'Hi, is that Mr Happy Pizzas? Can I order some lunch, please? Two triple-pepperoni with extra cheese, one triple-pepperoni with pineapple and grated chocolate, one anchovy pizza and one diet pizza with just tomato. Half an hour? That's great.' Oli gave his address and hung up.

'Your sisters have weird taste in pizzas,' commented Skipjack. 'I always think you can tell a lot about a person by the kind of pizza they like.'

'My sisters are weird full stop,' sighed Oli.

'There you go.'

Oli stood up. 'Right, wish me luck.'

'Good luck,' said Skipjack. 'Chuck us the phone and I'll call my mum to ask if I can sleep over. I don't want to miss *Real Blood Bath Murders*.'

Oli decided to start with Becky as she was less

likely than Tara to beat him up. On his way to the stairs he passed the kitchen and noticed that, for a room containing Sid, it seemed particularly quiet. So he popped his head round the door.

Although Oli had learnt by now not to lay bets on what Sid would do next, he would still have expected her to do whatever it was the right way up. So he was surprised to find her the right way down, with her head on the floor – on a nice big cushion – and her feet waving about where her hair should have been.

'Hi, Sid . . .' he began.

'You mean low Sid – ha-ha! I'm doing my exercises. Learnt this from a wandering hermit in the Hindu Kush. Gets the blood to the head. Two minutes like this and I'm bursting with brain-power.'

Oli could see for himself that it got the blood to the head. Sid's face looked exactly like a giant, genetically-modified tomato.

At that moment Becky wandered in.

Oli gulped. 'Er, Sid, this is my sister, Becky,'

Sid beamed upwards. 'Hiya, Becky! I'm Sid, your new mum!'

Oli winced. This was a more sudden presentation of the facts than he would have chosen. How would sister No. 1 react?

'Whatever,' shrugged Becky. She floated over to the fridge to extract a yogurt and a can of diet cola and wandered out again.

Phew. One down and one to go.

Oli approached the tree house with trepidation. The rope ladder was drawn up and the shutter firmly battened down over the little window. This did not bode well. Like a missionary bravely trying to make friends with jungle cannibals, Oli had the uncomfortable feeling that he was being watched. He knew that the tree house was dotted with spy holes – he and Tara had pressed out the knots in the planks together. It was also well equipped with peashooters – plus a good supply of ammunition – for firing through these holes at an enemy below.

'Tara? Are you in there?'

'Where's Mum?' demanded a fierce voice in reply. 'And who's the mad orange woman you came home with?'

'Her name's Sid. She's not mad, she's really nice. Come down and meet her.'

'I don't want to meet her. Where's Mum?'

'I'll tell you if you promise not to lose your temper.'

'Too late! I'm losing my temper! Why won't you tell me where Mum is?'

'Stop shouting,' Oli begged. 'Sid will hear you.'

'I'm not shouting!' shouted Tara. 'Just tell me!'

'Mum's gone out for a while. She'll be back later.'

'I don't trust you.'

'Well, you should. I've ordered you a Mr Happy pizza for lunch. Now will you come down?'

Silence. Then temptation:

'With anchovies?'

'Of course.'

'I'll come down when the pizza man arrives. I'm in the middle of rescuing Finbar.'

'Finbar?'

'A frog. I found him this morning by the back gate. Where the big puddle used to be, only now it's just a muddy hole. He was at the bottom, looking very dried up. I thought he was dead. I was going to dissect him but he twitched just in time. Now he's in a bowl of water.'

'A narrow escape for Finbar,' said Oli.

'Except I think now I might have drowned him.'

'I'm sure you haven't. You're great with animals.'

Silence. Then suspicion:

'Why are you being so nice, all of a sudden?'

'I've been nice before,' Oli said.

'Not this nice. And you still haven't told me where Mum is.'

Oli gave up. 'Well if you must know, I took her to the Mum Shop. Sid's a Replacement Mum. So there. I'll call you when the pizzas are here.'

'Don't bother. I'm not coming down till you get Mum back,' said Tara.

'Not even for pizza?'

'I'm going to stay up here and think of a horrible punishment for you.'

'With anchovies?'

'Go away before I shoot missiles at you.'

'How did that go?' asked Skipjack. He was lying on the grass trying to spin the basketball on his fingertips. Oli flopped down beside him.

'Becky didn't notice; Tara threatened to shoot me.'

'So, pretty much what you expected?'

'Yep.'

'Well, the good news is that my mum says I can sleep over.'

'Did you tell her Sid was here instead of Mum?' Oli asked him.

'No.' For the teeniest speck of time Skipjack looked guilty. Then he brightened. 'But I didn't tell her Sid *wasn't* here,' he pointed out.

Oli grinned. '*Real Blood Bath Murders* here we come!'

The crunch of tyres on gravel brought them both to their feet. Mr Happy! They ran through the house to open the front door. A beanpole of a lad in yellow uniform was standing on the doorstep, his chin resting on the stack of pizza boxes he was carrying.

'Pizza delivery,' he announced, just in case this wasn't clear.

'Yum-yum,' replied

Skipjack, eagerly relieving him of his load.

'That'll be £25, please,' said the lad.

'Hang on,' said Oli. He sped to the kitchen. 'Sid, can I have £25 for the pizzas, please?'

Sid looked surprised. 'But I haven't got £25. I haven't got any money.'

'But . . . How are we going to pay for the pizzas?'

'That's a good point,' agreed Sid. 'Haven't you got any money?'

'Just 25 p,' said Oli, remembering the last count. 'Skipjack?'

Skipjack put the pizza boxes down on the kitchen table, dug his hand in his pocket and pulled out a few coppers. 'Seven p. That makes 32 p. Not quite enough. What about Becky?'

'Always broke,' said Oli. 'Tara's got money but she never lends it; she's saving it to run away to Africa. What do we do now?'

'Can we think about that while we eat the pizzas?' asked Skipjack, eyeing the box marked 'Triple-pepperoni with pineapple and chocolate' and licking his lips.

'I've got some Monopoly money upstairs,'

suggested Oli. 'Do you think Mr Happy would notice?'

Skipjack giggled. 'We could throw in Mayfair and Park Lane.'

'And go straight to jail without passing Go,' Sid pointed out. 'No, we've got to be honest. And try to keep the pizza, too.'

A cough from the kitchen doorway made them all turn round. It was the beanpole. 'Er, can I have the £25 now, please?' he asked.

Sid took charge. She smiled at the beanpole warmly. 'Hiya! What's your name?'

'Er, Gavin,' said the beanpole warily.

'Hiya, Gavin! Gavin, we've got this little problem,' Sid began. 'We haven't actually got the £25 here and now. I mean, we have got it, but it's in the wrong place. I don't suppose you could lend it to us, could you? Just until tomorrow?'

The beanpole shook his head. 'The boss says we're not allowed to lend money. In any case I haven't got £25. The boss says if people can't pay we have to take the pizzas back.'

'No! Wait!' Desperate to stop her triple-pepperoni pizza with extra cheese from being driven away for ever in the back of Mr Happy's van, Sid tried one last time. 'I might have some money in my backpack. Hang on,' she said, diving in. 'Aha!' She drew out a tattered drawstring bag and shook its crumpled contents on to the table.

'Money!' she cried in triumph.

Everyone gathered round to look at the pile of notes. Oli picked one of them up. 'Not British money, though. Where's all this from?'

'Nepal, Bhutan and Tibet, mostly,' said Sid, squashing them back into the bag. 'But that doesn't matter, does it, Gavin? The important thing is that Mr Happy gets his £25. In fact, there's much more than £25 here. Mr Happy will make a big profit when he takes this lot to the bank.' She drew the strings tightly and held the bag out to Gavin but he eyed it with the gravest suspicion.

'I don't know if we're allowed to take foreign money,' he said. 'I think I should take the pizzas back instead.'

'What's the point in that?' asked Skipjack. 'You can't sell them to anyone else now, so they'll only be thrown away. Waste of pizza and no money for Mr Happy. This way the pizzas aren't wasted and Mr Happy gets lots of money. That makes much more sense, doesn't it, Gavin?'

Gavin scratched the back of this head. 'I suppose so.'

'Smashing,' beamed Sid. 'That's settled then. Goodbye, Gavin.'

So Gavin left, still looking very doubtful. Oli, Skipjack and Sid waved him off from the kitchen window before settling down at last for the pizza feast.

While they were munching, Oli and Skipjack told Sid all about their scary run-in with Mr Grimble on the bus and their plan for revenge. Sid roared when she saw the King Kong badge.

'What a smashing idea! That'll teach him to be such a big bully. Are you sure he entered the King Kong Look-alike Competition?'

'I'm sure he *didn't* enter it, cos there wasn't one,' said Skipjack.

'But he'll want to get a prize from the mayor,' Oli explained. 'So he'll go anyway.'

'You could change the letter,' suggested Sid,

'to say: "You have won the *secret* King Kong competition". So he'll know.'

'Know what?' asked Skipjack.

'Know why he didn't know he was in it. And what about telling him what time to turn up at the Town Hall? Then you can both go and hang around outside and watch him arrive. It would be a shame to miss it.'

'We'll have to go in disguise, of course,' said Skipjack.

Oli's eyes lit up. 'I can wear my dark glasses and my false moustache. He'll never recognise me in those.' He popped in another bite of pizza and chewed happily. Triple-pepperoni pizza, *Real Blood Bath Murders*, a brilliant anti-Grimble plan *and* a chance to wear his Secret Agent kit: life just couldn't get any better. He beamed across the table at his Replacement Mum.

'The Matcher was right about you, Sid,' he announced. 'You're lots of fun!'

Cedders to the Rescue

They were just finishing off the final crumbs of pizza when the driveway gravel crunched once more, followed shortly afterwards by a loud knock on the front door. Skipjack looked out of the window.

'The pizza van,' he told the others. 'Our friend Gavin's back.'

'I wonder what he wants,' said Oli as he went to open the front door.

On the doorstep stood Mr Grimble.

Oli nearly fainted with shock. 'M – Mr Grimble!' he stammered. 'What are you doing here? And why have you come in a Mr Happy pizza van?'

Mr Grimble looked as angry as a bull with a headache at a Liverpool cup final. 'Because I want my twenty pounds!'

'*You* are Mr Happy?'

'And you are the boy who wastes my time asking for bus tickets to Mars!' scowled Mr Grimble. 'I should have known it was you trying to pay for my pizzas with a load of funny money!' He thrust Sid's bag in Oli's face. Oli took a step backwards and blinked.

'Er, Sid,' he called. 'Can you come here? We've got a bit of a problem. It's Mr Happy. Only he isn't. Sid?'

Sid came bouncing to the door. 'Hiya, Mr Happy! What smashing pizzas those were. Is there a problem?'

Oli nudged her hard. 'This is Mr Grimble,' he

mumbled.

'Mr Grimble?'

Oli nodded.

Sid's eyebrows shot up. She looked Mr Grimble
up and down, then put her hand over her mouth
and leaned closer to Oli. 'King Kong?' she
whispered.

Oli nodded.

'I see what you mean!' Sid chuckled.

Mr Grimble was slowly turning purple. 'Yes,
there is a problem, a very big problem. The
problem is that you have just eaten stolen pizzas!'

'But they weren't stolen!' objected Skipjack, bravely popping his head through the kitchen door.

Mr Grimble spotted him. 'You!' he roared. 'The other Mars-boy! I might have guessed you'd be here. Those pizzas were not paid for with Proper British Money, and that makes them as good as stolen.'

'Didn't you like all my notes from Nepal, Bhutan and Tibet?' Sid looked hurt.

'No, I did not!' shouted Mr Grimble. 'And unless you can pay now, in Proper British Money, I'm calling the police.'

Sid looked at Mr Grimble sadly and then turned to Oli. 'We'd better go back to the Mum Shop,' she sighed. 'I can get the money there. I'm sure Mr Happy will give us a lift.'

'Well, hurry up, then,' chivvied Mr Grimble. 'I haven't got all day.'

'Oh, go and boil your bottom!' exclaimed Sid.

Mr Grimble's eyes nearly popped out of his purple face; he opened and closed his mouth a few times like an indignant cod in a fisherman's net. Finally he said, 'I shall wait in my van for exactly two minutes and then I shall drive straight to the police station.'

Oli closed the front door on him. 'It was a good try,' he said, handing the bag of money back to Sid.

'Some people are so stuck-in-the-mud,' said Sid. 'Ah, well,' she added with a sigh, 'I'd better pack.'

'Pack? Why?'

'You need a different mum. A sensible mum. I shouldn't have come. It's always a disaster.'

'It wasn't a disaster,' objected Oli. 'It was *fun*.'

But Sid shook her head. Even her hair seemed to have drooped. Then she chuckled suddenly. 'At least there's one thing to look forward to – the look on Cedric's face when he sees me back so soon!'

A question occurred to Oli. 'Why do you keep your money at the Mum Shop?' he asked.

'Oh, it's not my money – it's Cedric's. Cedric

has lots of money.'

'What makes you think he'll lend you any?' asked Oli.

'He won't want me to go to prison.'

'Why not? Why should he care what happens to you? He doesn't seem to care about anyone but himself.'

Sid smiled. 'Simple. He's my son.'

Oli's jaw dropped so low it nearly hit the floor. 'Cedric is your *son*?'

If Sid had told him she was really the Queen of England in disguise Oli could not have been more surprised. On the one hand there was Sid: large, bright and jolly, and on the other hand there was Cedric: skinny, pale and  miserable. Questions were queuing up in Oli's mind and the one that came out first was:

'How did he get that way?'

Sid shook her head. 'It's a mystery. I did everything I could to make him as normal as me.'

This was too much for Skipjack. 'Who is this Cedric bloke, anyway?' he wanted to know.

Just as Oli was telling his friend all about the bundle of joy that was Cedric Stringfellow, a loud hoot of impatience blasted from the pizza van.

'You'd better hurry,' remarked Skipjack, 'or Mr G will be off to the police.'

'Not him,' snorted Sid. 'However much he'd like to see us all behind bars, he wants his twenty quid more. He'll wait.' She started scooping her belongings off the kitchen table and squashing them down into her vast backpack.

Talking of £20 and watching Sid load up reminded Oli of two things. Number One: he was going to need another new mum and Number Two: unless she was on extra-special offer like Sid, she was unlikely to come free. He would need money. It was the same old problem. Oli ran upstairs to his room in search of something he could turn into pounds and pennies. How much did a new mum cost? There came a knocking sound from the back of Oli's brain, as if from a thought locked in a small cupboard there. Oli knew he could not ignore the thought for ever so he turned the key and let it out.

'What about getting your own mum back?' asked the thought.

What about it? Oli glanced at his watch. One-thirty. It had only been three hours since he had handed his mum in. To ask for her back after such a short time would be Giving Up on a cosmic scale. It would be like Christopher Columbus, having set sail to discover a New World across the ocean, turning back before he left the harbour because the sea looked a bit choppy. It was out of the question. His mum had to stay in the Mum Shop for at least one night. He would get her back tomorrow morning.

Oli returned his attention to matters of finance. Surely he must have something he could sell? As he searched the scrapyard of his desktop he spied with his little eye something beginning with c: his camera, just peeping out from under an old sock which had mysteriously crawled up there to die. Oli's heart sank because he loved his camera and really, really did not want to part with it, but he knew he had no choice.

Mr Grimble honked again.

Oli grabbed the camera and ran downstairs.

Keen to help his friend in whatever way he could, Skipjack offered to stay and Hold the Fort. Besides, there might still be a chance of watching *Real Blood Bath Murders* later.

Mr Grimble made Oli and Sid sit in the back of his van, saying he did not want to be seen giving a lift to low-life pizza-robbers. The van was empty of its usual cargo but the lingering smell of warm, crispy pizza made Oli and Sid feel hungry all over again. Oli tried to think of something else.

'How did Cedric end up running a Mum Shop?' he asked.

'He took it over from my dad, about five years ago,' explained Sid. 'Poor old Cedders – he's not cut out to run a Mum Shop. Brilliant with machines, but useless with people. They don't warm to him, maybe because he's about as much fun to be with as a bad case of chickenpox. I can say that cos I'm his mum. And there's another thing.' Sid's eyes narrowed in a puzzled frown.

'Something funny's going on at the Mum Shop. I keep warning Cedric about it but he won't believe me.'

'What sort of thing?' asked Oli.

'There are some suspicious mums around. They exchange glances all the time and nod meaningfully at one another. And they lurk. Sometimes I come round a corner and find a gaggle of them all whispering together. When they see me they stop and pretend to talk about the weather or something. I've even spotted them passing secret notes. It's very dodgy. I was in Kalamistan just before the revolution and I tell you, Oli, I had just the same feeling.'

'What's a revolution?' asked Oli.

'It's when everyone hates the big chief so they all gang up and chuck him out. In Kalamistan it was the workers who revolted. They were fed up with slaving away all day and not being paid more than a bag of beans. So they stormed the parliament building and murdered the prime minister. Then they sawed his head off and stuck it on the railings. It was not a pretty sight, I can tell you.'

'Was he a very ugly prime minister?'

'Very ugly. And very mean.'

'Do you really think the mums at the Mum Shop are plotting a revolution?'

'All I know is that there's Dirty Work Afoot.'

Oli thought it very unlikely that anyone would want to put Cedric's head on the Mum Shop railings, however annoying he was. Sid's whispering mums were more likely to be gossiping than plotting, perhaps about Sid herself, who was not exactly your regular kind of mum. The secret notes probably contained nothing more dangerous than 'Sid's a nutter – pass it on'.

The pizza van pulled up at the Mum Shop. Mr Grimble came round and opened the rear door a fraction.

'You can stay here until I get my £20,' he muttered through the crack.

He slammed the door on his hostages and his footsteps crunched away up the gravel path. It was pitch black in the van with the engine switched off. Sid and Oli waited. And waited.

'What's taking so long?' Oli wondered.

'Cedric will be making Mr Grimble fill in a form,' replied Sid, 'to say he's received the money and he's not going to have us arrested. Cedric loves getting people to fill things in.'

At last the footsteps came crunching back and the van door opened. Mr Grimble glared in at his prisoners.

'He wants proof that you're still alive before he hands over the money,' he growled. 'Anyone would think I was a bloomin' gangster. Out, both of you.'

They clambered out into the sunshine with relief. As Mr Grimble marched ahead Oli whispered to Sid, 'Cedric can't really think that Mr Grimble would do us in over a few pizzas, can he?'

'Of course not. That was just Cedric's way of putting off the painful moment when he has to part with a twenty-pound note. If filling in forms is Cedric heaven, handing over money is Cedric hell.'

As Oli came through the doorway into the hall he collided with a large, heavy object. Closer inspection revealed this blockage to be none other than Slugger Stubbins, school bully, teachers' terror and ruler of the junior rugby club. God created Slugger as a follow-up to the American bison and went on to perfect the design in the form of the rhinoceros. Colliding with Slugger was a risky business but this time Oli was in luck, for Slugger's tiny mind was already too full to send a message to his fist.

'Urgh,' grunted Slugger. 'It's you. Well, I'll give you some free advice: don't bother. That Septic bloke couldn't come up with one single mum for me. Not one. Said my requirements were too difficult. Idiot.'

As Oli stepped aside to let Slugger pass, he thought what a lucky day it was for all the mums in the Mum Shop.

Oli and Sid's arrival was greeted with a stinging look from Cedric, like a lemon squirt in the eye. Mr Grimble was standing by the counter with his arms crossed, glowering.

'See? Satisfied that I haven't chopped them into little pieces and sprinkled them on my Meat Feast pizzas? Now if you don't mind, I'll have that £20 this instant and without any further ado.'

Cedric unlocked his cash box, took out a crisp note and handed it over with distaste. Mr Grimble scrumpled it into his pocket and turned to leave but on his way out he paused to wave a fat forefinger at Sid.

'You should be ashamed of yourself!' he scolded. 'And as for you,' he added, turning to

Oli, 'I'm watching you, very carefully!' His final steely glare swept around the room like machine-gun fire and then he was gone.

Sid beamed at her son. 'Well done, Cedders! You saved the day!'

But the frost which coated Cedric Stringfellow was not to be melted by these warm words from his nearest and dearest. 'I do wish you wouldn't get yourself into these scrapes, Mother,' he remarked. 'It gives the shop a bad name.'

'Stuff and nonsense. Now then, you've got a job to do. My friend Oli here needs a new mum. Jump to it, Cedders!'

'Please don't call me that, Mother.' Cedric took a Replacement Mother Application Form out of a drawer and flapped it at his customer.

As Oli filled in the form, he wondered if he should make some changes from his last application. It was very important that nothing unexpected should happen between now and tomorrow morning, when he could bring this new mother back and swap her for his own mum. Maybe it wasn't a good idea to list 'being a secret agent' as one of his hobbies? But it was such fun to put that, and it couldn't make much difference, surely. The important bit to get right would be the Replacement Mother Requirements. The experience of being locked up in Mr Grimble's pizza van had taught Oli that asking for 'lots of fun' could land a boy in all kinds of trouble. This time he would have to be more careful. After a great deal of hard thinking he came up with:

1 Pizza once a day (paid for by replacement mum)
.2 Real Blood Bath Murders
3 Not too much fun

Oli sighed as he wrote number 3. It seemed such a waste of a golden chance, like having a free gift token for the biggest sweet shop in the world and only buying sugar-free mints.

Cedric uncovered the Matcher and pressed the big red frisbee button. While the great machine was going through its warm-up jerks he coughed meaningfully to get Oli's full attention and then puffed up his chest and spoke.

'I would like to make it completely clear that I

do not stock any further free Replacement Mothers and that, should you wish to take a mother away this time, you will have to pay for her in full before leaving the building. I assume you have brought the necessary funds with you?'

Oli correctly translated all this as meaning: No dosh, no mum.

'Well, I haven't brought cash exactly,' he said. 'I've brought this.' And he fished out his precious camera and placed it on the counter.

Cedric wrinkled his nose as if Oli was offering him the mouldy corpse of a dead rat.

'A barter?' he sniffed. 'That may be how my mother likes to buy things, but I'm afraid this is not some fourth-world flea market. We do not barter.'

Sid roared with laughter. 'Don't be so bloomin' pompous, Cedders! Every time I come back from my travels you've got worse.' A naughty gleam came into her eye. 'This makes me think,' she continued, 'that perhaps I shouldn't go away and leave you, ever again. Then you wouldn't have a chance to get pompous, would you, Cedders?'

Cedric glared at his mother. 'All right!' he

snapped. 'I'll take the camera. But it won't buy you a Class A or B mother. You'll be restricted to Class C and below.'

'How far down do the classes go?' asked Oli.

Cedric jerked his head at Sid. 'That far.'

Sid winked at Oli and drew a large 'Z' in the air.

'Feel free to go, Mother,' remarked Cedric, flicking the Turbo Boost switch.

'Thanks, Cedders,' called Sid above the Matcher's clanks and gurgles. 'But I want to make sure my friend Oli here gets a fair deal.'

'I think we can safely trust the Matcher to do that,' came Cedric's crisp reply.

'Why can't we cheat a bit, just to make sure?' asked Sid. 'There's a really nice mum in the room next door to mine upstairs –'

'Out of the question, Mother,' Cedric told her firmly as he fed Oli's form into the slot. 'The Matcher must decide.'

Dirty Work Afoot

Meanwhile, in a small room upstairs at the Mum Shop, Mother 44 was sitting at her computer, putting the finishing touches to the Revolution. The plan needed just one final check before it was sent out to the Comrades. Mother 44 began by reading the Mission Statement: 'To remove all Modern Nonsense from children's lives and bring back plain food, hard work and the Cane'.

The shrivelled heart of Mother 44 swelled with pride. This would put the spine back into youth and make the nation great again! Ever since she had started out as a science teacher all those years ago, Mother 44 (or Gertrude Swithin, to use her proper name) had watched as children grew more and more horrible. She had tried being strict with them, but it was no use.

The stricter she was, the more horrible the
children had become. The cause of all this
horribleness was as plain as the nose on
Comrade Olga's face. It was Modern Nonsense.
All that television, all those crisps. But as a

teacher, Gertrude Swithin had been powerless to
do anything about it. She was not allowed to use
the cane – she was hardly allowed to punish the
children at all.

Then one day, after she had given a
particularly horrible boy double detention for
letting off a stink bomb in her science lesson,
and then denying it, something clicked inside
her. If no one else would force these monsters to
behave, then she would have to do it herself. She

would be the superhero who defended the town against wickedness and stink bombs! She would be like Batman. Except that she wouldn't wear her underpants on the outside. She would seek out others who shared her vision and they would fight the fight together.

And so the Black Cane Brigade was born.

Gertrude Swithin read more of the Revolution Statement:

1 All junk food will be banned, including burgers, fizzy drinks, crisps, chocolate and pizza (especially pepperoni, which has been shown to cause extreme cheekiness in boys). Anyone caught eating any of these banned foods will be punished by Caning.

2 Children will be required to eat regular portions of the following: boiled cabbage, lumpy mashed potatoes (grey)

and fatty gristle.

3 All television will be banned, except educational programmes, which may be watched under strict supervision. However, educational programmes about ancient or tribal people who do not wear enough clothes will also be banned because of bare bottoms, which cause giggling. Giggling is also banned. Anyone caught watching television without supervision, or giggling, will be punished by Caning.

4 Also to be banned: computer games, electric guitars, remote-control toys and skateboards. Possession of any of these items will be punished by Caning.

5 Children will be banned from speaking until spoken to, except in emergencies, when

they must first raise their hand to receive permission to speak. Any child who speaks without either (a) being spoken to or (b) raising their hand and receiving permission to speak will be punished by Caning.

6 Children must wash behind the ears three times a day because that's what Comrade Olga had to do when she was a child and it made her what she is today. Regular checks will be made by trained Enforcers and failure to be completely clean behind the ears will be punished by Caning.

7 Scientists have firmly linked the rising number of horrible children with the fact that nobody eats milk pudding any more. This proves what those of us in the Black Cane

Brigade have always known:
milk pudding builds character!
Face a bowl of curdled junket
without fear and you can face
anything! Milk pudding of one
kind or another must therefore
be eaten daily. Tapioca,
semolina and sago are all
permitted but junket is best
because, being curdled, it is
even nastier than all the
others. Milk pudding will be
the superfood of the
revolution and the new
National Dish. From Junk to
Junket, Comrades!

Gertrude Swithin sighed. What a stirring slogan that was! The next section was headed 'Supply':

Several thousand new canes and
a reliable supply of milk
pudding will be needed.
Fortunately the Black Cane

Brigade has been contacted by a
'Mr Happy' (codename) who is
keen to help us. Mr Happy has
offered to sell his current (top
secret) business and set up a
milk pudding and cane factory.
Canes will be black to make them
scarier, and not less than 60 cm
long to maximise pain. Mr Happy
has been made an honorary comrade
of the Black Cane Brigade.

Control: Phase 1 was to recruit
parents and teachers to join the
Brigade. This has been very
successful and we now have a
network of agents and Comrades
in every school in the town.
We are now entering Phase 2,
which is to find children who can
be brainwashed into working for
the Brigade. These children will
be trained as agents, to spy on
their friends and keep us

```
informed of all bad behaviour.
When we have enough child agents
we will launch Phase 3 — the
Full Scale Attack.
Good luck, Comrades, and Good
Caning!
```

Gertrude Swithin smiled to herself. The plan was perfect. She clicked 'send' and for a moment cyberspace was filled with messages on the wing to all the Comrades of the Black Cane Brigade. Now all she had to do was sit back and wait to be matched with a child horrible enough to need some serious brainwashing, whom she could turn into a willing spy. And since Comrade Olga had hacked into the Mum Shop database, she did not expect to be sitting back and waiting for long. In order to maximise her chances of getting the perfect match, Mother 44 had asked for a boy with dreams of becoming a secret agent and a passion for pepperoni pizza.

Downstairs in the office, the Matcher finished matching and fell silent. Out popped a white card which fluttered to the ground.

'The Matcher has decided,' announced Cedric. He picked up the card. 'Mother 44.'

As Cedric pressed the buzzer Oli threw a questioning glance at Sid but she shrugged her shoulders. 'I don't know their numbers. I might recognise her when she appears, though.'

They heard quick heels on the stairs.

'Wow – that was fast,' remarked Oli.

'Mother 44 is very efficient,' Cedric told him. 'Not like some,' he added meaningfully.

The double doors opened.

When Oli saw Mother 44 he felt a surge of relief. For although he had not believed a word of Sid's talk about Dirty Work being Afoot, it was vital that this new mother should not cause any trouble before the next morning, when he could bring her quietly back and exchange her for his own mother again. One look at Mother 44 told him that trouble was the last thing on her mind. That same look also told him that the second last thing on her mind was fun, but Oli wasn't complaining. It was only for one day.

Mother 44 was tall and slim and very neat.

She wore black trousers, a
black shirt and black boots
and she carried just a
briefcase. She had straight
black hair and wore small,
round, wire-rimmed glasses.
She was clearly not a triple-
pepperoni mum like Sid and
her favourite TV programme
was unlikely to be *Real Blood
Bath Murders*, but she looked
the sort to say, 'Yes, you may,'
to any request so that she
could get back to counting
saucepan lids and sorting
soup tins alphabetically.

'Hello,' she said. 'You must
be Oli. I'm Mother 44.' She
held out her hand.

'Hello,' said Oli and gave it
a quick shake. It was cool and
dry, like snakeskin.

'Shall we go?' said
Mother 44.

'OK.'

Oli paused to say goodbye to Sid, who had been busy rummaging in her backpack and who was now scribbling something on the back of a scrap of paper. She wrapped this scrap around a small object and thrust it at Oli. 'Pocket!' she whispered.

Puzzled, Oli trousered the parcel. 'Bye, Sid,' he said.

'Cheerio, Oli my friend,' replied Sid soberly. 'I'm sorry I let you down.' She suddenly flung her enormous arms around him and squeezed him in a hug so tight that in a flash he knew how it would feel to be lunch for an anaconda. He was still gasping when he followed Mother 44 outside.

'The bus stop's just up there,' he said. He

thought of Mr Grimble and shuddered. Would his jailer be back on duty behind the wheel of the No. 11?

To his surprise, Mother 44 said, 'We don't need the bus.'

'We don't?'

'No. I've got transport,' she said, and with these three words she shot up Oli's approval scale and rang the bell at the top.

'It's just round the corner,' said Mother 44.

Oli was happily wondering what kind of car Mother 44 would have – a compact three-door city model, probably – when she said, 'This is it,' and stopped.

'This' was a small, armour-plated tank.

7
The Mysterious Mission of M44

Seeing the tank parked in the line of cars along the street was like seeing a giant alien in the school lunch queue. For a moment Oli's brain seemed to faint from the shock of it all and the only thing he could say was:

'It's a tank.'

'Yes,' said Mother 44. 'I'm just borrowing it from a friend while my car is at the garage. Follow me.' She slithered up the side of the tank and opened a hatch in the turret. Oli clambered up after her and peered down through the hole. There was a pair of seats directly below him.

'This is where you sit,' said Mother 44. 'Pull the hatch down when you're in and put on that headset so that we can talk to one another.'

She sprang down from the roof and opened another hatch in the bonnet of the tank.

'This is where the driver sits,' she explained, sliding in.

Oli lowered himself through his hatch and after a few painful knocks against sharp bits of tank he was in position. On either side of his seat was a lever studded with knobs and switches.

'What do these levers do?' he called.

'They're pistol grips. They control the guns.'

'You're joking!'

'I never joke.' She started the engine and they moved off.

Oli's brain was coming round now. As he settled down to enjoy his first ever tank ride it occurred to him that having Mother 44 around might turn out to be quite fun after all.

'What's your name?' he asked.

'You'd better call me M44.'

'Are you in the army?'

'Why would I be in the army?'

'Because of the tank.'

'I told you, my friend lent it to me.'

Oli smelt a rat. 'Where did you learn how to drive it?' he asked.

M44 hesitated for just long enough to be sure that Oli noticed, and then said, 'My friend showed me how to drive it.'

Aha! thought Oli – she's not telling the truth! Cunningly he asked, 'So, what kind of car do you normally drive?'

'Er,' said M44, 'it's a . . . a . . .'

Oli pounced. 'Don't you know?'

'Don't you believe me about the tank?'

'No, I don't.'

'Then you're just as clever as I hoped you would be.'

Of all the answers in the world, Oli had not expected this one. 'I don't understand,' he said.

'Then I'll explain. Can I trust you to keep a secret?'

'Yes!' said Oli eagerly.

'I need the tank for a special mission.'

Oli's heart skipped a beat. 'What kind of mission?'

'Top secret. The point is that we're looking for bright boys like you with special agent skills to help us.'

Oli gasped. 'Really?'

'Why else do you think the Matcher put us together? If you promise to help me, I'll make you my assistant. Special Agent Second Class. I'll even teach you to drive this tank. But remember, it's Top Secret.'

Oli's heart was leaping up and down inside him shouting yippee. For as long as he could remember, he had dreamed of being a secret agent. He had read books about spies and he had carried out practice missions on his sisters. Now here was someone actually asking him to *be* a secret agent on a real live mission.

M44 interrupted his thoughts. 'I should warn you that being a secret agent is hard work. You have to be physically fit – lots of exercise and no junk food. And you have to use all your powers

of concentration. That means nothing to take
your mind off the job – no telly or computer
games. And of course you have to be completely
obedient and follow commands straight away, so
that I know I can depend on you in an
emergency. Well? What do you say?'

So entranced was Oli by the vision of himself as
a secret agent that phrases such as 'no junk food'
and 'no telly', which would normally have crashed
into his brain like rocks through a window, merely
floated about like bubbles in his head.

'I say yes,' replied Oli without hesitation.

'I thought you would,' said M44 and smiled.

Skipjack had decided that Holding the Fort was
hungry work and was busy making himself a pile
of peanut-butter-and-chocolate-spread sandwiches
when a sound from outside made him glance
through the window.

A tank was rolling into the driveway.

Skipjack dropped everything and raced outside
in time to see his best friend climbing out of the
hatch.

'Oli! What are you doing in a tank? Have you
joined the army?'

Oli jumped down, grinning from ear to ear. Out
of a second hatch came a tall woman in black.

'Hi Skip – meet M44. M44, this is my mate
Skipjack.'

Skipjack took one look at M44 and had the same feeling that Ben Kenobi had when he landed on the Death Star and knew that Darth Vader was about.

'Are we a rebel outpost that you've come to wipe out?' he asked.

'Not exactly,' replied M44. Those eyes were like glacier mints. Skipjack shivered. There was something familiar about this woman, but where had he met her before?

'The tank's on loan from a friend,' explained Oli and winked at M44.

'Yes, but what for?' Then Skipjack had a brainwave. 'Hey, Oli, let's use it to attack Mr Grimble!'

M44 frowned. 'Who is Mr Grimble?'

Before Skipjack could tell her all about the King Kong of the Number 11 Bus, Oli, keen to place himself several miles away from such a silly idea, said, 'Be sensible, Skip. This is a serious piece of machinery, not a toy.'

Skipjack rolled his eyes. 'Lighten up, Oli. Can I at least have a go in it?'

'Maybe later,' said M44, in the voice that

grown-ups always use when they really mean: not in a thousand million years. She looked at the house. Yes, she decided, it would make a good headquarters for the Black Cane Brigade. She wondered if there was a nice big cellar for the Enforcers to work in. Naughty children could be so noisy while being caned, and she did not want any of them escaping before they could be fully subdued.

'I would like to see the house,' she told Oli.

'Follow me, M44,' said her Special Agent smartly and led the way.

Skipjack watched Oli lead M44 indoors with the feeling of doom that a sheep might have had on seeing Little Red Riding Hood direct the wolf to her grandmother's cottage. He sat down on the grass to think. His was a simple approach to life and he took things as they came. But when the thing that came was an armour-plated tank containing a best friend who had apparently been brainwashed and a woman who made you think of Darth Vader, you could not just take it. You had to think. So that's what Skipjack did.

In the hall, M44 turned to Oli. 'What a nice

house. It's very like my house, except my house has a cellar.'

'This house has a cellar too,' Oli told her eagerly. 'A really big one. We pretend it used to be a dungeon. It's got rings in the walls and everything.'

M44 smiled. 'Well, fancy that. Now, I would like to meet your sisters. Will you bring them to me, please?'

The mention of sisters gave Oli a start. He had entirely forgotten that he had sisters. He groaned inwardly. 'I'll get Becky,' he said and trudged off up the stairs with a heavy heart. Would M44 allow him to keep his Special Agent status once she knew the worst about his sisters?

When he reached the landing, however, Oli began to feel more hopeful. Becky's room was strangely quiet, which could only mean one thing . . . He opened the door and peeped inside. Yes, the room was sister-free. Becky was out! Phew!

He galloped back down the stairs two at a time. 'Becky's not there,' he told M44 happily.

'So I suspected when I found this coded note by the telephone,' she replied. 'Can you put your

deciphering skills to good use and crack it for me?'
She handed him a scrap of paper on which was
scrawled, in pink biro, 'S/o L – bk tom am – B'.

'She's gone to her friend Ella's for a sleep-
over,' Oli translated. 'She'll be back tomorrow
morning.'

'You have trained hard, I can tell,' said M44.
'You are going to be a valuable member of our
mission.'

Oli swelled like a proud balloon.

'And where is Tara?' continued M44.

'She's probably still in the tree house,' said Oli
carelessly.

'The tree house?'

'Yes. She said earlier that she wouldn't come
down until –'

Oops.

'Until what?'

'Until she was ready,' finished Oli.

'She sounds dangerously independent,'
commented M44. 'I shall deal with her later,
with an axe.'

This was alarming. 'Er, why an axe?'

'To chop down the tree, of course.'

'Of course,' agreed Oli, relieved. 'Silly me.'

'Now, run along, please,' said M44. 'I need to make a telephone call.'

'OK. I'm going up to change. I'll feel even more like a Special Agent if I'm wearing the right clothes.'

When Oli was safely upstairs M44 picked up the receiver and dialled.

'Hello?' croaked Comrade Olga at the other end.

'The Black Cane Brigade has a new headquarters,' said M44 in a low voice and she gave Oli's address. 'Tell the Comrades.' She replaced the receiver. Then she took her briefcase into the kitchen.

Outside, Skipjack was still sitting on his patch of grass and his thoughts had ambled to the matter of *Real Blood Bath Murders* when Oli emerged from the house and bounded in his direction.

Skipjack looked up. 'Oh, no!' he groaned and clapped his hands over his eyes.

Oli was dressed from top to toe in black. The black tracksuit bottoms, socks and trainers would

have been fine but over these he wore a very long
black roll-neck, which Skipjack guessed was
Becky's, and a wonky pair of black sunglasses.
His hair was slicked back with water. He was
wearing his false moustache.

But Oli, in his keenness to look the part, had
forgotten that he couldn't actually tell Skipjack
what that part was; he was not allowed to
mention the mission. Now, halfway across the
garden and having been spotted, he suddenly
remembered this important point. He stopped.

Skipjack, still covering his eyes, called,

'Tell me you are a mirage.'

'I had to change. I, er, got wet.'

Skipjack peeped through his fingers. 'Wet?'

'Yes. From water. Very wet water. And all my other clothes were in the wash.'

'And the moustache?'

Oli felt his upper lip. 'Well, how did that get there?' he exclaimed. He removed the moustache and stuffed it in his pocket.

Skipjack didn't really believe him, but on the other hand he didn't want to believe that his friend was turning into Darth Oli. So he tried to forget about the clothes. His eyes fell on the big lump of solid steel sitting in the driveway.

'I still say there's something dodgy about that tank,' he declared.

'I think it's cool,' said Oli. 'She showed me how to drive it. She said I was a natural and that I could be really useful in a national emergency.' He so longed to tell Skipjack about being made a Special Agent that he thought he would burst.

Something in Oli's voice made Skipjack feel the teeniest stab of jealousy. He changed the subject. 'What about *Real Blood Bath Murders*? Have you asked her?'

'Is that all you can think about?' Oli laughed with the superior air of one who has been chosen for higher things.

'It's the whole reason you got into this mess,' Skipjack pointed out.

'It's not a mess. It's an interesting experiment.'

'It's a mess,' said Skipjack. 'You've swapped one mum who nearly got us all arrested for another mum who drives a tank.'

'Come on, Skip! Where's your sense of adventure?'

'I don't trust her, Oli. When I look at her I hear Darth Vader music.'

'Why? Darth Vader never drove a tank.'

'Also I've met her somewhere before, I know I have.'

'Where?'

'I can't remember,' Skipjack frowned, 'but I know I didn't like her then, either.'

As they sat next to each other on the grass, silence fell between them like an iron curtain. Oli was disappointed. Here he was, on his first-ever mission as a special agent, a mission so top secret that he didn't even know what it was, and there was Skipjack, grumping on about Darth Vader. Skipjack was disappointed, too. It was as if his best friend had gone to another place and left him behind with the worrying question: had Oli been lured to the Dark Side?

8

Gertie Gets Going

Gertrude Swithin was not disappointed. Oli was
more willing than she could have dared hope. He
was like clay in her hands – she could make out
of him anything she wanted. She could easily
persuade him to spy on his horrible friends and
report their misdeeds to the Black Cane Brigade
Enforcers. She could even, she was sure, turn
him into a milk-pudding eater.

That friend of his would be a tougher nut to
crack. She had recognised Jack Haynes instantly
as the Stink Bomb Boy from her days as a
science teacher, and her right hand had itched
for a nice big cane. But whacking the Stink
Bomb Boy's bottom, however tempting and well
deserved, would have to wait until the Black
Cane Brigade were in control. Meanwhile she

had other plans for him. Plan A was for some speedy brainwashing. Plan B, the back-up plan, was to send him away.

The first step in Plan A was to win Skipjack's trust and to do this she would have to give him something he really wanted. With Oli this had been the promise of a secret mission, but to trap Skipjack she would have to spin a different kind of web. It was time to act.

Gertrude Swithin clicked open her briefcase. Inside lay the tools of the revolution: a portable computer, a black cane and two tins of

wholesome milk pudding – tapioca to be precise, the gloopy one full of little chewy lumps. Miss Swithin took out the tins and gazed upon them worshipfully. This, after all, was Official Revolution Food. Everything that the Black Cane Brigade was fighting for was summed up in these tins. No Modern Nonsense here – even the labels had not changed for forty years. With deep respect, Comrade Gertrude opened the tins and dolloped their innards into a large bowl. She found two smaller bowls and two spoons and set them out on the table.

Then she opened the kitchen window and called, 'Oli!'

'Yes, M44!' Special Agent Oli leapt to his feet and ran indoors to obey his leader. His friend, left alone on the grass, sank even further into gloom. If Oli had a tail at the end of his bottom, thought Skipjack, he would be wagging it hard. Who was that woman in the kitchen and what was she doing here? Skipjack knew she was up to no good. If only he could remember where he had seen her before.

'Here I am, M44,' panted Oli.

'Good. You can remove your dark glasses now. Oli, I am pleased with your performance. Everything is going according to plan. But before we can proceed we need to deal with the problem of Skipjack.'

'Problem?'

'Problem. He senses that we have a secret.'

'He knows something's up,' agreed Oli.

'My instinct tells me he should leave now, before he endangers our mission.'

Oli's face clouded over.

'It is a shame that he does not like me,' continued M44, 'because with your expert help he could become a good special agent and help us in our mission. You would like to have Skipjack as your assistant, wouldn't you?'

'It would be great,' agreed Oli. 'But you're right, M44: He doesn't like you. I can't think why.'

'Neither can I,' sighed M44. 'Oli, if you could make Skipjack trust me I would promote you to Special Agent First Class.'

'A promotion!' Oli beamed. 'Would that mean I could tell Skipjack about the mission?'

'First I would have to set you both a little test, as proof,' said M44 in a voice as light as a sprinkle of icing sugar.

'What kind of test?'

M44 indicated the bowl brimming with spotted, jelly-like mucus.

'Frogspawn!' exclaimed Oli. 'Where did you find it? Are we going to hatch frogs? Is that part of the secret mission?'

M44 struggled to be patient. 'Not frogspawn, Oli. Tapioca. It's a tapioca test.'

Oli's face fell.

'Our organisation recommends that all our agents eat regular quantities of milk puddings,' M44 told him. 'They contain special vitamins and minerals that increase strength and brainpower. If you can eat a whole bowl of tapioca and if you can persuade Skipjack to do the same, then I will know that you possess great leadership powers and that Skipjack is worthy of joining us.'

Oli looked at the tapioca doubtfully. He knew he had more chance of getting Skipjack to send a valentine card to Slugger Stubbins signed with love and kisses than to eat one spoonful. On the other hand, he wanted M44 to let his friend stay. And he wanted to become a Special Agent First Class.

'I'll try,' he said, 'but it's not going to be easy.'

'Just think of that promotion,' M44 told him.

On his way outside Oli racked his brain for the best way of persuading Skipjack to tackle the tapioca. His brain-racking was interrupted in the hall by the telephone ringing. He picked up the receiver.

'Hello?' he said, and then added as an afterthought, 'Special Agent Oli here.'

'Then that must be the Headquarters of the Black Cane Brigade?' asked a voice.

'The what? Oh, yes, I suppose it must be.'

'Let me speak to Comrade Gertrude.'

'To who?'

This must have been the wrong thing to say. There was a long silence from the other end followed by a click. The line went dead.

The Black Cane Brigade? Comrade Gertrude? . . . Puzzled, Oli continued on his journey to the front door where he almost bumped into Skipjack hurrying in.

'Come outside,' whispered Skipjack urgently. 'I've got something to tell you.' Curious about the reason for Skipjack's new excitement, but fairly sure it was not the sudden realisation that he worshipped M44, Oli followed him back into the garden.

As soon as they were out of earshot of the house Skipjack turned to Oli. 'I've remembered where I've met her before,' he whispered.

'Where?'

'At school. She was a science supply teacher for a week. Her real name's Miss Swithin. You must remember – she gave me two detentions for letting off a stink bomb.'

Oli did not want this to be true. 'Are you sure?' he asked.

'Of course I'm sure,' said Skipjack with feeling. 'I don't easily forget people who make me write 200 lines of: "Boys who throw stink bombs in Miss Swithin's science lessons should be drowned in a bath of H_2SO_4".'

Oli thought about this. Finally he asked, 'Wouldn't you dissolve before you drowned?'

'That's not the point!'

'Well, if you let off stink bombs you've got to take the punishment.'

'It wasn't even my stink bomb that time,' objected Skipjack. 'It was Slugger's.'

The mention of Slugger Stubbins gave Oli a good opportunity to change the subject.

'Talking of Slugger, you'll never guess where I saw him this morning?'

'Where?'

'In the Mum Shop!'

'He'd be a good match for your precious M44.'

So much for changing the subject. Oli sighed.

'M44's really sad that you don't like her, Skipjack. She wants us all to be friends.'

'I can't be friends with anyone who looks like Darth Vader and dishes out detentions willy-nilly,' said Skipjack firmly.

Oli was beginning to despair of ever being promoted to Special Agent First Class when he had a sudden flash of inspiration.

'If you can't get on with M44,' he said, 'it's going to be difficult for you to stay and watch

Real Blood Bath Murders.'

Oli had struck gold. If there was one thing Skipjack wanted to get out of today it was the rare chance to watch *Real Blood Bath Murders*. There was a long silence while Skipjack's mind chewed this over thoughtfully.

'I suppose I could pretend to like her, just for tonight,' he conceded at last.

Oli's promotion was still within reach. 'That's the spirit, Skip! We might have to pretend we like her cooking, too. Just for tonight.'

'I suppose so.'

There would never be a better time for the tapioca test. Oli took a deep breath.

'Talking of which,' he continued, 'I think she's made us something to eat already. Are you hungry?'

Skipjack was always hungry. He suddenly remembered his uneaten peanut-butter-and-chocolate-spread sandwiches and came willingly to the kitchen, where the first thing he saw, apart from Darth Vader with a bin bag, was a big bowl containing fish eyes in glue. Skipjack looked at Oli questioningly.

'It's tapioca,' said Oli brightly and then he murmured out of the corner of his mouth, 'think of *RBBM*.'

Skipjack glanced at the counter where he had left his peanut-butter-and-chocolate-spread sandwiches. They were gone. He had a bad feeling about this.

'Where are my sandwiches?' he asked.

'Oh, were they yours? I've thrown them away,' announced M44, dropping three bags of prawn-cocktail crisps and a packet of chocolate-chip cookies into the bin bag.

The bad feeling grew worse. 'Why?'

'That kind of food isn't good for you, Jack,' said M44. 'That's why I've made you and Oli a bowl of tapioca. Oli's going to eat it, aren't you, Oli?'

Oli nodded eagerly. 'Yes, M44. Tapioca contains special vitamins and minerals that increase strength and brainpower. You should try some, Skipjack.'

Skipjack shook his head. 'No, I shouldn't.'

'*Please*,' begged the Special Agent Nearly First Class.

'No!' cried Skipjack. 'What's got into you, Oli? Why are you sucking up to her like this? You're like some creepy android!'

Oli flushed angrily. 'I am not!'

'What about your own mum?' Skipjack demanded. 'Sitting in the Mum Shop waiting for you? Have you forgotten all about her?'

Oli glared angrily at Skipjack, but M44 spotted the shadow of guilt which crossed his face. Plan A had failed and if she didn't act fast Oli would be un-brainwashed. It was time for Plan B.

'Oli,' she said briskly. 'I have tried my hardest

to put up with your friend but it is clear that he has decided to hate me. The situation cannot continue. Either he leaves or I leave; it is time for you to decide.'

Oli looked from Skipjack to M44 and back again miserably. He opened his mouth to say something and then he closed it again.

'Don't worry, Oli,' said Skipjack in a grim voice. 'I'll decide for you. I'm going. I couldn't stay a second longer, anyway. Goodbye, Oli. Goodbye, Miss Swithin. I wish you death by a thousand stink bombs.'

With his head held high, Skipjack marched out of the kitchen.

M44 turned to Oli. 'You must forget him, Oli. He was standing between you and your destiny.'

'He was my friend,' said Oli sadly.

'He was angry and jealous. A true friend would have rejoiced at your talent and good fortune. Come along, Agent Oli. We have work to do. We have a mission to accomplish!' She slapped him on the back in a comradely way.

But Oli drew away from her. 'First tell me what the Black Cane Brigade is,' he said.

'It's just a code name,' said Gertrude Swithin. 'It doesn't mean anything.'

'The code name of the mission?'

She clicked her tongue. 'Yes, the code name of the mission.'

'You still haven't told me what the mission is.'

'All in good time. For now you only need to know that it is of national importance.'

Oli shook his head. 'I can't go on helping you without knowing what it's about.'

Her eyes narrowed behind their wire spectacles. 'What's the matter, Oli – don't you trust me any more?'

Suddenly Oli saw what Skipjack meant. The black clothes, the enormous height, the shiny boots and the helmet of straight black hair: she was just like Darth Vader. 'No,' he said. 'I don't. I want to stop being a special agent. I want to take you back to the Mum Shop and I want to get my own mum back. I want to be friends with Skipjack again.'

There was a long silence. Finally M44 said in a cold, hard voice, 'I am afraid it's too late for all that.'

Oli gulped. 'What do you mean, too late?'

'I cannot allow you to stop now. You know too much. You have no choice but to obey. And I would advise you to be as co-operative as possible. You see, our organisation can access the Mum Shop computer system. If you make any trouble at all, I will simply instruct my comrade there to match your mother with –' she paused – 'Slugger Stubbins.'

Oli gazed at her in speechless horror.

'You have thirty minutes to make a decision,' M44 told him. 'Either you are with us, or your mother pays the price.'

9
Double Agents and Triple Knockout Drops

Oli dragged himself outside, his head spinning.
He had made a complete mess of everything and
he hadn't a clue how to sort it all out again.
Worst of all, he had driven his best friend away,
just when he most needed an ally. What an idiot
he had been. Now he had nobody at all to help
him, unless . . .

He approached the tree house, scanning each
knot-hole for protruding pea-shooters.

'Tara?'

'Go away.'

This was not a good start.

'How's your frog?'

'Finbar's dead.'

'Ah. Oh dear.'

'I dissected him,' said Tara. 'I've found out
how frogs poo.'

'At least he didn't die for nothing.'

'No. Lovely new Mum, Oli.'

It was no time for false pride. Oli took a deep breath. 'Tara, I need help. She's crazy. She wants me to be a spy. She's trying to brainwash me. Can I come up?'

'No.'

'Can you come down, then?'

'No.'

'You're a heartless sister, Tara.'

'Yep.'

'I might be murdered. Don't you care if I'm murdered?'

'Me coming down isn't going to stop you being murdered. It just means I might get murdered, too.'

'Well, why can't I come up, then?'

'Don't be silly. How can you ever get Mum back if you're hiding up here?'

Clear-headed logic is normally a fine quality to see in your sister. But not when you are stranded under a tree house, within tapioca-spitting distance of Comrade Gertrude from the Black Cane Brigade. It was time to play the card

Oli hoped would be his winning ace.

'If we don't stop her she's going to get Mum handed over to Slugger Stubbins.'

'That would be all your fault.'

'Oh, *please* help,' Oli begged.

'I'm not coming down and that's final!' shouted Tara.

Oli glared up into the tree. 'When I've been brainwashed to death, I'll come back and haunt you!' he yelled.

'Good! I'll like you much better as a ghost!'

Feeling miserable and very alone, Oli wandered down to the end of the garden. He leaned heavily on the gate and gazed unseeingly at the beautiful spring afternoon. He wished there was a Sister Shop. Then, he heard a voice.

'Psst! Oli!'

Oli spun round, alarmed. Was this the rest of the Black Cane Brigade coming to get him?'

'Over here,' hissed the voice.

It appeared to be coming from a violently rustling bush. Even Oli, with his limited experience of revolutionaries, knew that you couldn't hide a whole brigade of them in one bush. Feeling a little less anxious he went over and peered into the vegetation.

He came face to face with Skipjack.

'Skip! What are you doing here?' cried Oli. Bells of joy were pealing in his heart.

Skipjack grinned. 'I couldn't leave you to your doom.'

Oli was deeply moved. 'Thanks, mate. Sorry.'

'Don't worry about it. She's a psycho, Oli.'

'You don't know the half of it,' muttered Oli, glancing over his shoulder towards the house.

'But how are we going to get rid of her?' asked Skipjack.

'Let's go and hide behind the shed and make a plan.'

'Good idea. This is a very uncomfortable bush.'

'It's a holly bush.'

'That would explain it. Ouch.'

Oli kept watch on the house while Skipjack crept out of his prickly hiding place and scuttled across the grass to the back of the garden shed. Oli joined him a second later and checked his watch.

'I've got twenty minutes left,' he said.

'Until what?'

'M44's gang have hacked into the computer at the Mum Shop. She says she'll get my mum matched up with Slugger Stubbins if I don't agree to help her.'

Skipjack rolled his eyes, staggered about and keeled over backwards, pretending to faint. Then he sat up again. 'She'll have to wash his rugby socks,' he said in an awed voice. There was a shocked silence. The Stubbins rugby socks were famously horrible. In fact, Slugger himself often boasted that they were more powerful than a nuclear bomb. To prove this, he could clear a packed playground in seconds by rolling his odious footwear into a ball and firing it from his catapult while shouting, 'Socks!'

'And she'll have to let him watch *Real Blood Bath Murders*,' Skipjack went on. 'I bet Slugger Stubbins always gets to watch *Real Blood Bath Murders*.'

'I bet Slugger Stubbins has the starring role,' grunted Oli. 'Question is, how can we stop M44?'

'Can we lock her up somewhere?' suggested Skipjack. 'It would have to be somewhere without a window so she can't escape, like your cellar.'

'Then what?'

'Then we call the police.'

Oli gave a hollow laugh. 'What, and say, "Excuse me, officer, but we have the leader of the Black Cane Brigade locked in our cellar. We would like you to come and take her away. And while you're about it please move her tank which is blocking our driveway"?'

'I see what you mean,' agreed Skipjack. 'They might not believe us.'

'No, we need to get her back to the Mum Shop ourselves,' said Oli. 'And for that we'll have to overpower her, or double-cross her, or both. But how?'

'I wish Sid was here,' sighed Skipjack. 'She would help us.'

'Sid!' Oli slapped his forehead. 'She gave me something in the Mum Shop – I forgot all about it!' Oli dug into his pocket and pulled out a very small parcel rolled up in a crumpled sheet of paper. He unwrapped it and came to a tiny bottle. On the back of the paper Sid had scribbled, 'Look out – she's one of them!' The two boys looked at the label on the bottle:

Good old Sid.

In the kitchen, Gertrude Swithin was sitting at her computer typing an order to Comrade Olga to arrange the match between Oli's mum and

Slugger Stubbins. She was confident that Oli would agree to act as a spy but she had decided to send the order anyway. Oli's fondness for his own mum could endanger their whole mission; the woman had to be placed safely out of reach.

Oli came into the kitchen. Gertrude Swithin clicked send, closed the computer and looked up.

'Well? What is your decision?'

'I want to stay with you, M44,' said Oli, trying to look humble yet keen. 'I'm sorry about that business with Skipjack. I was all muddled. Of course he's not my friend any more.'

'I am delighted to hear it.'

'I'll do anything you ask,' continued Oli earnestly, 'as long as you let me stay as your assistant.'

'I can see I was right to select you, Oli.' M44 even managed a smile but it was a stiff, creaky smile and Oli could tell it had been dragged up from somewhere deep inside and dusted off for the occasion.

He beamed back at her. 'Thank you, M44. I think we should both have a bowl of tapioca to celebrate!'

The smile vanished.

'I want to be full of strength and brainpower for the mission ahead and I expect you do, too,' continued Oli. He began ladling the tapioca into the two bowls on the table.

'I think that's enough, don't you?' suggested M44 through gritted teeth as she watched the bowls filling up.

'One more for luck!' said Oli happily. He scooped out another spoonful which he managed to slop across the lid of M44's computer.

'Now look what you've done!' she exclaimed crossly and she hurried to the sink to fetch a cloth. Her back was only turned for five seconds but it was enough time for Oli to unscrew the bottle of knockout drops, tip the whole lot into M44's bowl of tapioca and stir it in.

'I'm really sorry,' said Oli, watching her wipe the computer lid clean. 'I was just so excited about the mission.'

'You must learn not to be so careless,' she told him as she placed her computer safely on the dresser.

'Yes, M44. Can we start now?'

'I suppose so.'

Oli told Skipjack later that he had no memory at all of getting outside his bowlful of tapioca. He had been too busy watching M44 eat hers and hoping that the knock-out drops would work. There had been no instructions on the label, so the boys had agreed to use the whole bottle, just to be on the safe side.

Oli glanced across the table. Was he imagining it, or was M44 looking a bit dopey? He glanced again. Yes, the head was nodding, the eyelids were drooping, the body was beginning to sway. M44 made one last effort to lift the spoon but it was useless – she was no match for Sid's Ping Yong knock-out drops. The spoon fell to the floor and M44's head slumped forward on to the table. She was out cold.

Oli leapt to the window. 'Skipjack!' he yelled. 'It's worked!'

Skipjack appeared from behind the shed pushing an ancient wheelbarrow which he trundled towards the house at top speed, shouting 'Ner-noo ner-noo ner-noo!' He came clattering through the back door and along the corridor and appeared triumphant in the kitchen. 'Here's the Blood Wagon!' he shouted.

'Let's load her in.'

Puffing and panting, the two boys hauled M44 off her chair and dumped her in the wheelbarrow.

'I'll get a blanket from upstairs,' said Oli. 'You grab her briefcase.'

A minute later the two boys were wheeling the unconscious leader of the Black Cane Brigade down the drive, hidden beneath a tartan rug. But fate was waiting round the corner to spike their plan: one moment the barrow was bouncing along with ease, the next moment there was a pop from below and an ominous hiss. The boys looked down at the wheel. It was flattening fast, while on the pavement just behind them lay the tell-tale glass shards of a broken bottle.

'Oh no,' groaned Oli. 'Now what?'

'We could take her in your go-kart?' suggested Skipjack.

'You crashed it last week – remember? Trying to break the land-speed record down Skid Hill.'

'So I did. Sledge?'

'In case you hadn't noticed, there isn't any snow.'

'So there isn't. I know – how about borrowing a shopping trolley?'

'The nearest supermarket is about a hundred thousand light years away.'

'That would put it in the next galaxy,' Skipjack pointed out.

'OK, maybe not quite that far. But too far for us. We can't hang about, Skip. We don't know when she'll wake up.'

'In that case,' said Skipjack, 'there's only one thing for it. We'll have to take her in the tank.'

Tanks a Lot

Oli stared at his friend.

'You're not serious?'

'What else can we do?' asked Skipjack. 'Unless you've got a forklift truck up your sleeve?'

'You *are* serious.'

'She showed you how to drive it. You said it was dead simple,' Skipjack reminded him.

'It is. Two pedals – stop and go. Two levers – left and right. That's it.'

'So, what are we waiting for?'

A slow grin spread over Oli's face.

'You'll have to let me drive it too,' Skipjack added.

'Of course,' promised his friend.

'There's just one thing,' said Skipjack. 'How are we going to get the old bag into the tank? We can't drag her up the side – she's too heavy.'

Oli thought hard. 'I've got it!' he exclaimed. He pointed to a tree near the driveway. It happened to be the one containing the tree-house, and therefore also Tara. Oli would have preferred a Tara-less tree – in fact right now he would have preferred a Tara-less life – but that couldn't be helped.

'See that branch?' Oli said in a low voice to Skipjack.

'What are you talking about?' called Tara. 'I've been watching you both through my spy-holes. You're going to do something crazy, I can tell. You'll probably end up in prison. Or worse.'

'It's nothing to do with you, traitor,' shouted Oli. He turned back to Skipjack. 'We'll hang a rope over that branch,' he whispered, 'and tie one end round M44's middle. Then we pull hard on the other end and she'll go up in the air. Then you keep holding our end of the rope to keep her up there and I get the tank and position it so she's hanging above the hole. Then you let go of the rope and she drops down the hole. Get it?'

'Got it.'

'Good. I'll go and find a rope.'

Oli dashed to the garden shed and disappeared inside. There came the sound of a horde of excited Vikings going berserk in a saucepan shop. Oli came out again, panting.

'Just the thing!' he called, waving a long, thick piece of rope.

Together the boys rumbled the wheelbarrow over to the tree and tipped its contents out on to the grass. Then Oli flung the rope over the branch.

Tara's furious voice shouted, 'What are you doing with that rope?'

'We're going to tie one end to the tank and pull your tree down,' called Oli. 'Unless you shut up.'

Tara was silent.

'It worked!' chuckled Oli.

He tied one end of the rope round M44's waist using a tangle of knots that Skipjack was sure they would never be able to undo without a very sharp sword. Then they began to heave.

'I don't want her up here!' called Tara. 'Take her down!'

'Did you say something?' asked Oli, hauling

on the rope. 'Because if you did, we'll have to pull the tree down.'

Tara was silent again.

'If only I could keep that tank,' sighed Oli dreamily, 'I'd never have trouble with her ever again.'

'I wish we had one of those catapults they used in the old days to fire rotting cows into castles,' panted Skipjack as their heavy load began to inch skywards. 'We could just aim Miss Swithin at the hole and ping! Off she'd fly.'

'You'd have to be a very good shot,' puffed Oli. 'There, I think she's high enough. Are you ready to hold on while I get the tank?'

'No,' panted Skipjack.

'I've just thought of a problem,' puffed Oli.

'There's always a problem,' panted Skipjack. 'What is it this time?'

'The key to the tank is still in her pocket.'

So M44 was lowered on to the ground again. Skipjack rubbed his aching shoulders as he watched Oli extract the key. 'Why don't you check you can start the tank and make it go backwards and forwards before we haul her up again?' he suggested.

'Good idea,' agreed Oli. 'Are you coming in or staying out?'

Skipjack considered. As this was Oli's maiden voyage, the tank was sure to crash into something or roll over, which made being inside it seem rather unsafe. On the other hand, if he stayed outside the tank he might end up being the thing it crashed into or rolled over, which would be even more unsafe. The best option was to be outside, but not too close and ready to run. There would be plenty of time to join in the tankery once Oli had got the hang of it.

'Staying out,' he said, 'Just so you can concentrate better on your first go.'

'Yeah, right,' grinned Oli.

He jumped down the driver's hatch. This was going to be fun.

The seat was positioned so that he could close the hatch and look out through the periscope. But M44 had shown Oli how to raise the seat so that he could drive with his head sticking out of the hatch and he decided this would be good fun. He adjusted the seat and then turned the key in

the starter. A pleasing chug came from the
engine. On either side of his seat was a lever. If
he sat on the edge and really stretched, he could
just reach the foot pedals. He put the tank into
gear and eased the levers forwards. It moved!
This was great! He shifted the right-hand lever a
bit and the tank turned slightly until it was facing
in exactly the direction of the tree.

'Here I come!' he called and Skipjack gave
him a thumbs-up in reply. Oli moved the tank
forwards . . . and forwards . . . Now, where was
the brake?

'Stop!' yelled Skipjack in alarm, leaping away like a jet-propelled bullfrog. The tank stopped.

'Sorry! I forgot how to brake!' shouted Oli cheerfully.

'You nearly flattened the whole tree!'

'Rubbish! I had inches to spare.'

'You did that on purpose!' yelled Tara.

'I was keeping you on the ball,' Oli told her.

The boys began the great heave all over again. Slowly the sleeping M44 rose higher and higher until she was swinging gently in the breeze just below the branch. Then Skipjack held on while Oli raced back to the tank and in a trice was inching it forwards again until their captive's feet were hanging just over the top hatch.

'Awesomely perfect!' he cried.

'Can I drop her now?' begged Skipjack, whose feet were beginning to leave the ground.

'Not yet,' replied Oli cheerfully. 'We've got to make sure all her arms and legs go in, or she'll just go splat on top. Skipjack! I said don't drop her!'

But it was too late. M44 went splat on top.

'I didn't drop her – she pulled me up!'

Sure enough there was Skipjack, dangling
among the leaves.

'I don't want him up here, either!' yelled Tara.

'Hey, Skip, you're quite high!' said Oli,
impressed. 'You'll have to let go and do a
paratrooper's roll.'

Skipjack let go.

'Any damage?' enquired Oli as his friend lay in
a crumpled heap on the ground.

'Only my arms,' groaned Skipjack. 'They must be about six inches longer after all that stretching.'

While Skipjack checked that his knuckles were not in fact grazing the ground, Oli untied the rope and shoved M44 down through the top hatch. She landed in the tank with a clatter. As Skipjack climbed in next to her, his eyes fell on the pistol grips.

'Hey, these look cool. What are they?'

'Don't touch those! They fire the guns.'

'Awesome! Are they loaded?'

'I don't know and we're NOT going to find out,' said Oli firmly.

'Spoilsport.'

'We'll close the hatches and use the periscopes,' said Oli, handing him M44's briefcase to put on the floor. 'Then people will just think there are soldiers inside. You have to put on that headset so we can hear each other.' He climbed into the driver's hatch.

'I knew you were going to do something crazy,' called Tara. 'You'll definitely end up in prison. Or else you'll be shot or blown up.'

'Shall we pull the tree down now?' Skipjack asked.

'It's very tempting,' said Oli through gritted teeth. 'But we'd better get going.'

'Don't forget we're swapping seats halfway so I can have a go driving,' said Skipjack before he closed his hatch.

'I won't.' Oli settled into his seat, adjusted his headset and peered through the periscope. 'Ready? Action Stations: We will now advance on the Mum Shop!'

He found reversing a bit tricky so he drove round in a big circle until he was back on the driveway and away they went, very slowly. Much too slowly for Skipjack.

'Come on Oli – give it some welly!' he urged. 'At this rate we won't reach the Mum Shop till Christmas. Are you going to take the short cut? You turn right just up ahead. It's much quicker.'

'OK. Right, did you say? Here we go . . .' Oli slowed down to almost nought miles an hour and brought the tank carefully round the corner. He found himself facing a brick wall.

'Great short cut, Skip.'

'Why did you turn left? I said turn right.'

'I did turn right.'

'Oh. Oops. I meant left. I always get them muddled. Sorry, Oli. I guess you'll have to get the hang of going backwards now. Or shall we knock this wall down?' he added, hopefully.

Fortunately for anyone who might have been enjoying life on the other side of the wall, Oli managed to reverse the tank. Soon they were back in the street, rumbling slowly along and giggling at the surprised looks on people's faces. They might have reached the Mum Shop quite peacefully if Skipjack had not insisted on having his turn at the wheel. Oli tried to put this off for as long as possible, partly because he was having such fun driving the tank himself and partly because he knew his co-pilot was a Master of Destruction. Oli remembered how Skipjack had reduced the go-kart to a heap of splinters at the foot of Skid Hill; he shuddered to think what his friend could achieve with a tank.

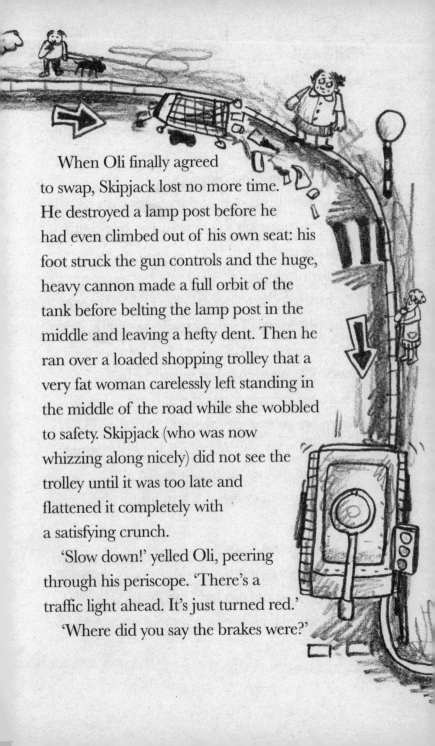

When Oli finally agreed to swap, Skipjack lost no more time. He destroyed a lamp post before he had even climbed out of his own seat: his foot struck the gun controls and the huge, heavy cannon made a full orbit of the tank before belting the lamp post in the middle and leaving a hefty dent. Then he ran over a loaded shopping trolley that a very fat woman carelessly left standing in the middle of the road while she wobbled to safety. Skipjack (who was now whizzing along nicely) did not see the trolley until it was too late and flattened it completely with a satisfying crunch.

'Slow down!' yelled Oli, peering through his periscope. 'There's a traffic light ahead. It's just turned red.'

'Where did you say the brakes were?'

'Skipjack!'

'Ha-ha – just kidding.'

Skipjack stopped.

The tank echoed with the sound of someone knocking.

'Come in!' shouted Skipjack.

Oli opened his hatch and looked down. A little old lady was banging the side of the tank with her walking stick.

'Er, can I help you?'

The little old lady looked up. 'Oh, there you are,' she observed. 'I saw you run over that poor woman's shopping. You never even stopped.'

'Sorry. We were in a hurry,' said Oli.

'That's no excuse for bad manners.'

'We're on an urgent mission,' explained Oli. 'Please tell her to send a bill for her shopping to Miss Swithin at the Mum Shop.'

'Where are you going that's so important, then?'

'To Kalamistan,' said Oli.

'Then you're going the wrong way. Kalamistan is that way,' said the old lady firmly and she pointed with her stick. She squinted up at Oli.

'You look too young to be going on missions.'

'I'm twenty-one,' he said.

'Are you really? You look about half that age. I wish I knew your secret for looking so young.'

'Pepperoni pizza,' Oli told her.

'Is that right? I'll have to try it. But then, when you're as old as I am everyone looks young. Like that constable coming along this way.'

Constable! Help! Was this traffic light never going to change?

At last it was green.

'Go, Skip, go!' cried Oli, ducking inside and pulling the lid down. He looked through his rear periscope as they rolled away. The policeman was bending to listen to the little old lady's chatter and looking curiously in their direction, like a giant question mark in black uniform.

The last thing Skipjack hit was the Replacement Mother Agency sign, which got in the way of his attempt to park the tank on the Mum Shop lawn.

Oli was out first and noted the damage: big black sign badly crumpled; smooth green grass deeply rutted; long muddy skid mark.

'Cedric won't like this,' he commented.

'He will if we tell him we nearly parked in his front room,' said Skipjack. 'I'm looking forward to meeting the lovely Cedric.'

The lovely Cedric greeted Oli with his usual charm.

'It's you, yet again,' he grumbled. Skipjack he ignored altogether.

Oli looked wounded. 'Please, Cedric, is that any way to welcome an old friend?'

'You are not an old friend. You are trouble.'

'Well, I like that!' exclaimed Skipjack. 'First you sell him a mum who nearly gets us all thrown into prison, and then you sell him a dangerous plotter who tries to brainwash us, and you have the nerve to call *Oli* trouble!'

'What dangerous plotter?' demanded Cedric.

'Mother 44,' Oli told him. 'She was part of a whole gang of plotters called the Black Cane Brigade. Didn't you know? They've been plotting away like anything right here under your nose.'

'You really should be more careful, Cedric,' added Skipjack. 'Imagine what the police would say if they knew the Mum Shop was really a safe house for plotters?'

'That's ridiculous!' snapped Cedric.

'Don't worry, Cedric. We promise not to tell,' Skipjack assured him. 'As long as you help Oli get his mum back.'

'That's right, Cedric' smiled Oli. 'I just want my mum back.'

'What have you done with your present mother?' Cedric asked. 'You can't swap her if she isn't here, you know.'

'M44? She's asleep outside,' Oli explained.

'Asleep?'

'Asleep,' said Skipjack. 'It's very tiring being a plotter.'

'Hmm.' Cedric looked from Skipjack to Oli and back again with narrowed eyes. He didn't trust them. But then, he didn't trust anybody. And he did want them to go away. 'All right,' he said at last. 'You can try to get your own mum back again.'

'What do you mean, "try"?' asked Oli.

'I mean that you have to go through the usual procedure. The Matcher must decide.'

A Friend in Deed

Skipjack nudged Oli. 'Who is the Matcher?' he whispered.

'It's not a who, it's a what,' Oli told him. 'A machine.' He lowered his voice. 'Cedric thinks it rules the universe.'

'There is also the question of payment,' said Cedric.

'You've already got my camera,' Oli reminded him.

'I'm afraid that won't be enough. Your mother is a Grade A Mother. If you want her back, you will have to come up with more than an old camera.'

Under most circumstances, Oli would have been chuffed to be the owner of a Grade A mum. But these were not most circumstances. Once more the dreaded money monster was rearing its ugly head, like a big blue troll clambering on to the bridge, smelly and slobbering and shouting, 'Just you try to get past.'

Skipjack tried to help. 'Don't you think,' he asked Cedric, 'that after all the trouble Oli's had with mums from your shop you can give a discount?'

Nobody who knew Cedric well would ever have asked him a question beginning with the words 'Don't you think' or ending with the words 'give a discount'. Cedric did not think at all – he just followed the rules. And he had never given anything in his life. So he said,

'No.'

Oli sighed. 'The only other thing I've got that's worth anything at all is my watch.'

'Let me see it, please.' A claw was held out.

Oli undid his watch and handed it over sadly. He loved his watch nearly as much as his camera. It was a deep-sea-diving watch with luminous hands and a stop-watch. Oli had never quite been deep-sea diving but he liked to know that if he ever did, he would be able to time the fish to see which was the fastest. Cedric examined every detail of the precious timepiece. Finally he said, with a cold glance at Skipjack, 'It will be enough, if you add his watch, too.'

As a friend, Skipjack had his faults. He was dangerously fond of speeding in tanks and he never had any money when you wanted to buy a pizza. But in other ways he was the best sort of friend a boy could have. He took off his watch and laid it on the counter.

'Cedric, you are a vulture,' he said.

'Thanks, Skip,' mumbled Oli.

'Fill this in, please.' Cedric placed the familiar blue form in front of Oli and went over to the Matcher. Skipjack watched with interest. He knew a boy whose dad kept an Aston Martin under a sheet like that. He could tell from the bulky shape that this sheet was not hiding an Aston Martin, but still Skipjack had that happy sense of excitement he used to get at magic shows just before the rabbit was pulled out of the hat.

Off came the sheet and Skipjack was not disappointed. The huge multicoloured machine with all its shiny levers and dials looked full of promise. He couldn't wait to see it in action.

Oli, meanwhile, stood at the counter chewing his pencil and wondering what Replacement Mother Requirements would match him with his own mum. Finally he wrote:

1 Pizza once a week
2 TV at the weekends
3 Quite a lot of fun

When Cedric came to collect the form Oli asked, 'Can I try again if it doesn't work this time?'

'It is possible, yes,' replied Cedric.

'As often as I like?' asked Oli hopefully.

'Certainly not. You have three chances. After that the Matcher will not accept any more applications from you for another twenty-four hours.'

Oli's form disappeared into the Matcher and the show began. Skipjack enjoyed it all, especially the really loud turbo-powered bit when the whole room shook, and when the little white card popped out at the end he nearly clapped.

'The Matcher has decided,' announced Cedric.

'Well?'

'Mother 28.'

'Mine?

'No.'

Oli sighed. 'Another form, please.'

After even more pencil-chewing Oli tried:

1 Chinese takeaway on the first day of the holidays
2 Watch me in my rugby matches
3 Let me and Skip sleep in the tent all night with a campfire

Five minutes later:

'Well?'

'Mother 57.'

'Mine?'

'No.'

Sigh. 'Another form, please.'

Everything depended on this final attempt. Oli had to think of even more things that were typical of his mum, but he was running out of ideas.

Skipjack was hovering nearby but he couldn't really help, and as there was only so long you could watch even the most fascinating person stare into space and chew a pencil, he took himself off on a voyage around the waiting room. He paused to admire the large green potted plant in the corner. There was a small window behind this captive speck of rainforest. After a quick glance over his shoulder to check that Cedric wasn't looking, Skipjack opened the window a tiny crack and then continued on his tour, a picture of innocence.

Back at the counter Oli had eaten nearly the

whole pencil, but with chewing had come inspiration. The Requirements were ready at last:

1 Fried breakfast on Saturdays
2 Let me climb trees and make arrows with my penknife
3 Just sort of stick up for me

'Keep everything crossed,' he told Skipjack as Cedric fed the form into the Matcher.

'Fingers, toes and eyes?'

'And all the bits in between.'

Five minutes later, out popped the card. Oli gripped the counter.

'Well?'

'No matches at all,' Cedric told him.

Oli drooped. 'That's it, then.'

Skipjack patted him on the back. 'No, it isn't,' he said. 'We'll come back tomorrow. And the next day if we have to. I'm sure that if Cedric knows we're going to be back every single day until we get a match he'll make it as quick as possible, won't you, Cedric?'

'There is nothing I can do to affect the outcome,' sniffed Cedric, wishing very much that there was. 'The Matcher must decide.'

Skipjack rolled his eyes. 'Yeah, yeah. Goodbye, Cedric. Come along, Oli.'

When they were safely away from the Mum Shop, Skipjack turned to his gloomy friend.

'Cheer up,' he grinned. 'I've got a plan.'

Skipjack's plans were nearly always mad, often bad and occasionally dangerous to know, but they were always worth hearing.

'Go on,' said Oli, brightening a little.

'We break into the Mum Shop tonight,' Skipjack announced, 'and get your mum back. How's that?'

Oli beamed like a torch with new batteries. 'It's brilliant, Skip! It's the best idea you've ever had. But how are we going to get in? The place is bound to be locked up and alarmed.'

'I had a good look round just now and I couldn't see an alarm,' said Skipjack. 'As for getting in, I opened a little window behind that plant in the waiting room. We'll just have to hope that Cedric doesn't notice.'

Oli was full of admiration. 'You're a much better secret agent than me, Skip,' he said, and he really meant it.

Not having the courage to take the bus, they walked back to Oli's house, making plans all the way. Oli kept a look-out for the little old lady with the walking stick who might have been surprised to see him back from Kalamistan so soon.

'Shame M44 threw all the nice food away,' commented Skipjack when they arrived back in Oli's kitchen. 'I'm starving.'

'There might be a pizza in the freezer,' said Oli.

'Good idea. Where's the freezer?'

But Oli did not hear. He had spotted M44's computer on the dresser.

Ah-ha! Now they could find out what she was really up to. He opened it up and the first thing to appear on the screen was a list of sent e-mail messages. Oli clicked on the most recent and read it:

```
Hail Comrade Olga!
I am making good progress with
the Biggles boy but until he is
fully brainwashed we must put
```

his mother out of the picture.
Please arrange immediately for
her to be matched with Slugger
Stubbins on the Mother
Replacement Agency system.The
house here will make an
excellent Brigade headquarters,
with a cellar ideal for
Enforcement. Please inform the
other Comrades.
Comrade Gertrude

'The old cow!' exclaimed Oli. He wondered whether this Comrade Olga person had carried out M44's instructions yet – perhaps his mum had already gone to Slugger Stubbins! Oli felt a swell of panic and forced himself to take a deep breath. No, Cedric would have told him if his mum had left. She must still be at the Mum Shop, but if she was not rescued quickly . . . An image of stinking, crusty rugby socks lurched into Oli's mind and he shut his eyes. The idea was too horrible for thought.

Oli searched further and found an icon called Revolution Statement. He clicked it.

Meanwhile Skipjack's homing device had led him to the freezer where he had found a nice big cheese and tomato pizza. He was now happily exploring the fridge for things to put on it and sharing his discoveries, he thought, with Oli: 'No pepperoni but lots of salami. We'll have salami instead. And bacon – I love bacon.'

As Oli read the Revolution Statement of the Black Cane Brigade, he shuddered to think how narrowly he had escaped. No telly, no junk food, canes and more canes – what kind of nutcase would dream up such a plan?

'Would it be greedy to have ham as well?' wondered Skipjack.

The really scary part for Oli was how easily he had been turned into M44's willing slave, just with one tank-driving lesson and the empty title of Special Agent Second Class.

'Tomatoes, sweetcorn, salami, ham, sausages, bacon, gherkins and cheese. Now that's what I call a pizza. It would be even better with chocolate on top but she's thrown that away. Never mind. In it goes.'

Of course, there was nothing to stop M44 from brainwashing other victims. Plus, how many more Black Cane Brigade members were out there doing the same?

'We must stop them,' Oli said aloud. 'But how?'

'Pizza's bubbling,' announced Skipjack, peering into the oven.

'If M44 is chief comrade,' said Oli, 'we must get her removed first, to some place where she can't do any damage. Then we must put the rest of them out of action.'

Oli thought and thought, and just as he felt his

brain would burst, he realised that the solution was right in front of him. He grinned to himself. First he brought the message to Comrade Olga back up on the screen. Then he changed it.

Dear Comrade Olga,
I have brainwashed Oli Biggles and he is now working for us. He is a trusted comrade and an awesome tank driver.
   Now I want a bigger job. Please go into the Mum Shop system and get me matched with Slugger Stubbins. Telephone him anonymously and tell him to come to the Mum Shop first thing in the morning to collect his perfect mother.
   One other thing. Our gang has been infiltrated by enemy spies who want to destroy our revolution. I have worked out a cunning plot to expose them. You must secretly tell all our

<u>trusted</u> comrades to stop the
mission at once and to start
saying that pizza is
fantastic. That way we will
know that any agent still
banging on about tapioca will
be an enemy spy. Clever, eh?
Comrades must go on eating
pizza until I tell them to
stop — I expect it will take a
long time to find all the
enemy spies. For extra
security you must never
mention this top secret
Operation Pizza to me again,
in case one of the enemy spies
overhears. Of course, we know
that I'm not an enemy spy so I
will go on brainwashing
Slugger as usual.

Please ignore any other
messages you have had from me
telling you to match anyone
else with Slugger Stubbins.

```
They were not really from me,
they were from the enemy
spies.
Comrade Gertrude
```

Still grinning, Oli clicked send. Then he closed down the computer and sat back.

'Now, what about that pizza?' he asked.

Midnight Mission

Anyone who happened to be passing the Biggles house later that night would have seen two very suspicious-looking characters sneaking out of it into the moonlight. Both wore dark clothes and had faces blackened with boot polish. One carried a backpack. The pair of them jumped on to bicycles and pedalled away in the direction of town.

The Mum Shop was in complete darkness, with

the tank still parked on the grass outside. The boys
leaned their bikes against a shadowy side wall and
then Oli climbed up the tank very quietly and
peeped inside. The leader of the revolution was
still with the fairies, but she was beginning to stir.
By morning she would be back to her old
revolting self. Oli took her computer out of his
backpack and put it in the briefcase beside her. He
then placed in her pocket a note which he and
Skipjack had composed over their pizza:

> Dear M44,
> Thanks for everything. Sorry, but
> while we were enjoying our
> tapioca Skipjack sneaked up
> behind you and hit you on the head
> with a cricket bat. He is like a
> madman. It is not safe for you to
> stay at my house any more. I
> hope you come round soon. I
> promise to be a good spy.
> Love from Oli.

This done, the two boys crept to the waiting-
room window. Had Cedric locked it? Luck was

smiling down on them with the moon; the window was open.

Oli and Skipjack had planned every detail of Operation Rescue Part 1 while waiting for the hours to pass until the town would be asleep. Now the two of them worked together like twin cogs in a well-oiled machine. Underneath the window, Skipjack locked his fingers together in a stirrup for Oli's foot. Oli stepped up neatly, pushed the window wider open and climbed inside. Then he picked up one of the waiting-room chairs and passed it out through the window for Skipjack, who used it to climb inside.

They made their way through the double doors at the end of the room to the stairs beyond. Long experience of nocturnal expeditions had taught Oli and Skipjack that there

was no such thing as a silent flight of stairs. There was always at least one creaky step, usually about halfway, just when you had begun to relax. The stairs in Oli's house had a chronic case of the creaks – every step could catch you out in a different place – and the boys had learnt the hard way that the safest place to tread was usually the very edge of the step nearest to the wall.

At the top of the stairs their plan became a little woolly. They were now entering the unknown territory of Operation Rescue Part 2. They had expected a corridor and doors and had sort of hoped that every door would be helpfully named, or that a quick peep into each room would locate Oli's mum. What they had not expected was such a long corridor and so many doors, all exactly the same and, as Oli discovered after cautiously trying the first few, all firmly locked.

Oli's hopes, which were on their last legs anyway, collapsed on to the floor. On the other side of one of these doors, perhaps only a few metres away, was his mum, yet she might just as well have been on the other side of an ocean. For a wild moment he even considered knocking on the first door and asking whoever answered for directions. But what if he got Cedric or Comrade Olga? It was too risky. The situation was looking hopeless.

But wait a moment: Comrade Olga . . . Oli frowned, racking his brains. Then his face cleared. He knew what to do. Tugging at Skipjack's arm he pulled him back down the stairs. Once they were on the slightly safer side of the double doors he explained the new plan in hurried whispers.

'The computer,' he hissed, nodding in the direction of Cedric's desk. 'We can find out Mum's details from the database. Then I'll know exactly what to ask for when I come back tomorrow.'

'Great,' Skipjack whispered. Ten tiptoeing seconds later Oli was switching on Cedric's computer. Fortunately it was an efficient machine and after a few blinks it was wide awake and ready to help. Fortunately Cedric was also an efficient machine and had clearly named all his documents, so it was the work of seconds to find the one Oli wanted. He clicked 'Mothers' details'.

Unfortunately Cedric was also a suspicious fusspot and he had protected 'Mothers' details' with a password. Oli uttered one of the swear words that carried a hefty fine at home; Skipjack uttered a swear word Oli had never even heard of and he made a mental note to ask him about it later.

Oli typed into the password box every variation of Cedric's name, from the full and formal 'Cedric Stringfellow' to the shortcut 'CS', but all were rejected.

'Try "Really Annoying Idiot",' suggested Skipjack.

'What could he have used?' Oli wondered. 'I never thought I'd say this, but I wish I'd spent more time chatting to Cedric about his interests.'

'I don't believe Cedric's got any interests,' said Skipjack, 'apart from his precious Matcher over there.'

Oli's eyes gleamed. 'Nice one, Skip!' He typed 'Matcher' in the password box and crossed his fingers. Nothing. Then inspiration hit: he remembered something Cedric had told him about the machine at their very first meeting and he typed in 'JumboJet'. It worked! He was in!

At the very moment that Oli was typing the words 'Jumbo Jet', an alarm clock was buzzing beneath Comrade Olga's pillow. This devoted member of the Black Cane Brigade had been shocked to learn, from Comrade Gertrude's email, of its infiltration by enemy spies. She had spent a busy evening spreading the message about Operation Pizza to the trusted comrades. Now it was time to get up and follow the other instructions in Comrade Gertrude's message. She had to go downstairs to the database and match up her dear leader with Slugger Stubbins.

Comrade Olga switched off the alarm, heaved herself out of bed, shoved her hairy feet into her moth-eaten slippers and set off.

Oli found his mum's page and

scrolled quickly down to her Requirements:

```
1 No rude jokes or cricket
  indoors
2 No TV on schooldays
3 Daily fruit and vegetables
```

He sat back with a sigh. He'd done it. What a –
CREAK!

'The stairs!' hissed Skipjack. 'Someone's
coming!'

There was no time to shut the computer
down. Oli pulled the plug out of the socket
while Skipjack looked around frantically for a
hiding place.

'The Matcher!' he squeaked. They dived
under the sheet and had just flattened
themselves against the far side of the machine
when they heard the slight sound of the double
doors being opened.

Comrade Olga padded across the moonlit
office to Cedric's desk and sat down. She
plugged the computer in, started it up, and
entered the password: JumboJet. She located
the requirements of Slugger Stubbins, which

were as follows:

1 New Mum must never tell me off
2 New Mum must let me practise
   rugby tackles on her
3 New Mum must let me do
   anything I want and give me
   loads of money

Comrade Olga sighed and shook her head. Her dear leader had chosen wisely when she had requested this match. The Stubbins boy was clearly in serious need of complete brainwashing. Comrade Olga had thought as much when she telephoned him earlier, following Gertrude's instructions, to tell him his perfect mother was awaiting collection first thing in the morning. He had been most offensive and rude. Operation Pizza had made Comrade Olga very sad, but she cheered up at the thought that the one child who would still be brainwashed was Slugger Stubbins. She quickly accessed Comrade Gertrude's details and changed them to match Slugger's. She was about to shut down the computer when a loud clank from the darkness made her leap up in a spectacular burst of flight.

Comrade Olga was not built like a grasshopper but an Olympic judge with a tape measure would have confirmed that this particular jump put 88 centimetres between her feet and the floor.

After the clank came bleeps and bangs and flashes of light – the Matcher was coming alive! With a gasp of horror Comrade Olga was out of that office and up the stairs like a bat out of hell, convinced that something supernatural was occurring.

What was in fact occurring was nothing more supernatural than

one of Skipjack's little accidents. The boys had
been standing statue-still under the sheet, waiting
for whoever had interrupted them to leave, and
trying not to breathe in the sudden smell of
cabbage soup. Then Skipjack had got a nasty
cramp in his left foot. While hopping about
trying to de-cramp, he had bumped into Oli and
pushed him against the big red frisbee button.

The boys were as shocked as Comrade Olga
when the Matcher started clanking. For a second
they froze in horror, convinced they would be
found. Then they heard her stampeding away
and they saw their chance to escape.

'Quick! Let's get away from here!' cried Oli,
fighting his way out of the sheet. They legged it
to the window and scrambled through, pulling it
closed just as the lights flickered on inside.

As Oli lay in bed that night, trying not to hear
Skipjack snoring on his camp bed a few feet
away, he did a quick recap in his head.

1 M44 would wake up soon and find
   his note. She would read it and

believe that she had succeeded in turning him into a Black Cane Brigade spy. So she would not suspect him of any anti-Black Cane Brigade activity.

2 She would also think that Skipjack was a dangerous lunatic. She would never forgive him for hitting her over the head with a cricket bat, but that couldn't be helped. Hopefully Skipjack would not have to face her in a science lab again.

3 In the morning Comrade Olga would tell M44 that she had carried out her instructions about being matched with Slugger. M44 might be surprised at first, but she would just think that the reason she didn't remember sending this message was that she had been knocked on the head. Everyone knew that people often went a bit fuzzy in the memory department after a bang on the nut. Also, there would be no

other explanation: she would never suspect Comrade Olga of anything naughty and she wouldn't suspect Oli either because she would think he was a good guy (see 1).

4 Slugger would come and collect M44 in the morning, believing that she was his perfect mum. When he saw the tank and heard about the Secret Mission he would go on believing it. And as he was really thick he would go on believing it for ages.

5 Comrade Olga would be busy making sure all the other comrades stopped the mission and started eating pizza.

6 The kids in Oli's town would be saved from the evil Black Cane Brigade.

7 Best of all, he would collect his own mum in the morning.

What were her requirements again? No rude jokes or cricket indoors, no TV on schooldays, daily fruit and veg. What horrible requirements –

no wonder he hadn't thought of them.

All in all, thought Oli, I've sorted everything out awesomely.

He threw a pillow at Skipjack to stop the snoring, rolled over and went to sleep.

The boys parted at Oli's gate the next morning. Skipjack cycled home while Oli set off on foot for his final visit to the Mum Shop. There was a spring in his step and a song in his heart; the sun was shining and the birds were singing. And to make a glorious day even more glorious, what did Oli spot when he happened to glance down at the ground? A five-pound note. Oli was an honest boy and the first thing he did on picking up the money was to look around to see if someone might have dropped it. He was honest but, as we know by now, completely broke, so he was delighted to find that there was nobody about at all. Then he realised that right in front of him was a flower shop. It seemed like destiny. He hesitated for only a second before diving into the shop and he emerged a moment later, having exchanged the fiver for a bunch of pink flowers.

When he reached the Mum Shop a few minutes later he was surprised to find a police car parked outside. So full of happiness was Oli that for a moment he completely forgot that he and Skipjack had spent the previous evening breaking and entering. And here he was, returning to the scene of the crime. He was halfway up the path when his subconscious, which luckily *was* paying attention, sent him an urgent picture of lions prowling around a den, which stopped him in his tracks.

He had just decided to leg it to the nearest tree, behind which he could lurk until the coast was clear, when two large policemen marched out of the Mum Shop. They were flanking a stout woman with beady eyes and the hint of a moustache. As the trio passed him, Oli's nostrils were bombarded by the violent smell of cabbage soup. The whole party piled into the waiting police car and drove away.

Oli continued up the path, relieved and thoughtful.

Once inside the Mum Shop, he remembered that he was only minutes away from getting his mum back and even the sight of Cedric looking extra-specially sour could not cloud his sunny outlook.

'Hello, Cedders!' he said warmly. 'Isn't it a beautiful day? Who was that going off with the coppers?'

'That was Mother 13,' scowled Cedric. 'I caught her last night hacking into the computer system and trying to sabotage the Matcher. She has been arrested. Not that it's any of your business.'

'How right you are, Cedders,' smiled Oli. He laid his pink flowers on the counter. 'I've just come to get my mum back.'

'Well, you're too late. She left ten minutes ago with a new client.'

Oli's heart lurched and his knees buckled. He clutched the counter.

'Who?' he asked faintly.

'I cannot tell you. That would be against our regulations.'

Oli slid down to the floor and sat there in a heap. One name kept swimming in and out of his head: Slugger Stubbins.

What if Comrade Olga simply hadn't believed the message he had sent? What if she had come down last night to match Slugger not with M44, but with his own mum, as instructed in the original message from M44 herself?

Oli became aware that Cedric was prodding him with a sharp foot. 'Get up, get up,' Cedric was saying. 'You are making the shop look untidy. Please leave.'

Oli scraped himself off the floor, picked up his flowers and left. For a while he walked in a daze, without knowing where he was going. Then the fresh air slowly cleared his foggy mind and he realised his feet had brought him close to the Stubbins house. He decided to sneak up and see if his mum was there.

As he sneaked, keeping low behind the hedges, he wondered just what he would do if she was.

He could try the direct approach and simply say, 'Hi, Slugger, can I have my mum back?' but Slugger would just say no and probably thump him.

He could try the indirect approach and attract his mum's attention without Slugger noticing.

But even if he helped her escape, Slugger knew where they lived. He would just come and get her back and *definitely* thump him.

As he crept round the last corner before Slugger's house Oli sighed. There seemed no way of getting his mum back without being hospitalised on the way. Then he stopped. There, neatly parked in the driveway, was the tank.

Phew! M44 was there after all!

But where's Mum? wondered Oli as he turned away. Who could the Matcher have put her with? He remembered her horrible list of requirements and shook his head, mystified. What kind of weird kid asked for daily fruit and veg and no rude jokes?

Oli would never have believed that such a kid existed in the whole world. How was he going to find it? He could try hanging around all the vegetable shops in town. No, that was ridiculous.

I've run out of ideas, thought Oli sadly. My brain is empty. I'll just go home and hope for a miracle.

Ten minutes later Oli walked into the kitchen and there, sitting at the table with Tara, was his mum.

A great surge of delight filled him to bursting.

'Mum!' he cried, rushing forwards. She gave him an enormous hug. He remembered the pink flowers he was still clutching and he handed them, crushed and battered, to his mum.

'Thank you,' she smiled. 'They're beautiful.' She looked around the kitchen. 'And it's so tidy. You've looked after everything very well while I've been gone.'

Oli reddened.

'No, I haven't. But we cleared it all up in the end.' He shot an anxious glance at Tara but she winked and grinned. She was all right, really.

'How did you get Mum back?' he asked her.

Tara shrugged. 'It was easy. I just thought of things that were true about Mum but that no one would ever ask for. I figured she wouldn't want to go anywhere else.'

That evening, Skipjack rang.

'Hi, Oli. Is she back?'

'Hi, Skip. Yeah, she is.'

'Guess what we forgot last night?'

'I dunno. Tell me.'

'We forgot to watch *Real Blood Bath Murders*!'

'After all that!' groaned Oli.

'But here's the good news: guess what's on tonight?'

'What?'

'*Real Chain Saw Massacres*! All the guys at school watch it. I thought maybe you could ask your mum . . .'

'Skipjack! Are you crazy?'

'Just one teenee-weenee askee? I know you

want to see it, really.'

'Bye, Skip.'

'No, wait – everyone says it's really unscary. There's almost no bloo–'

Click. *Brrrrrrrrrrrrrrr.*

'Oli! Bedtime!' Mum came into the hall. Oli was still standing by the phone. There was a far-away look on his face. Perhaps, after all . . .

'Mum, can I stay up a bit later tonight?'

'It's late enough, Oli. It's bedtime.'

'Only, there's something on TV I'd quite like to watch. All the guys at school watch it.'

There was a long pause. Oli could see that his mum was thinking. Perhaps she regretted being so hard-hearted about *Real Blood Bath Murders*. He smiled at her winningly.

'Oli,' she said finally.

'Yes, Mum?' he whispered, breathless with hope.

'Did you know there was a Kid Shop in town?'

'Argh! Goodnight, Mum!'

Oli Biggles leapt up the stairs, two at a time.

Loose Ends

Note on Oli's pillow that night:

You owe me LOTS of money for getting Mum back. I won't be able to run away to Africa for years now. So start saving. Or else.
Tara

Email to Olga Omsk from Gertrude Swithin, two days later:

Hail Comrade Olga!
I am making excellent progress
with Slugger, considering his
mental limitations. I have made
him Special Agent Second Class
and he is spying on all the boys

in the street. Why aren't you
replying to my emails?
Comrade Gertrude

Postcard to Gertrude Swithin from Olga Omsk,
three weeks later:

Dear Gertie,
The police let me go at last but I had to leave the country.
I've come home to Kalamistan. If you ever get away from
Slugger you must come and visit. I will show you the
monument to the workers' revolution and take you to the best
cabbage soup stand in town. Think what fun we will have.
Olga.
PS The police confiscated my computer so don't send any
emails or they might arrest you as well.

Letter delivered to Oli Biggles with a *Mrs* Happy
super-size triple-pepperoni pizza with extra
cheese and a parcel containing one camera and
two watches:

Hiya Oli!
Guess what – I've bought Mr Grimble's pizza shop! He was

selling it to set up a milk-pudding factory. Of course I didn't tell him that nobody eats milk pudding any more – except Cedric!

Talking of Cedders, you'll never guess where he went when he closed down the Mum Shop. I'm not supposed to say anything cos it's top-top hush-hush, so I'll whisper it: He's working for the secret service!! They found out about the Matcher and decided it was just what they needed for matching up spies with international criminal masterminds, but Cedders wouldn't let them have it unless they took him on to operate it. He spends all day in a cellar, matching away and hardly having to talk to anyone! He's never been so happy.

Thanks for the good times, Oli my friend, and keep eating the pizzas!

Lots of love,

Sid

Letter to Mr Grimble's boss at the bus station, from the Mayor:

Dear Sir,

I think you should know that your bus driver Mr Grimble appeared at the Town Hall on Saturday wearing a large green badge with I AM KING KONG written on it and demanding a prize. He is clearly potty and should not be allowed anywhere near a bus. You must give him a nice safe job pushing the tea trolley until he is back to normal.

Yours faithfully,

Sir Henry Widebottom

Mayor